George Chetwynd Griffith

The Romance of Golden Star

George Chetwynd Griffith

The Romance of Golden Star

ISBN/EAN: 9783337049041

Printed in Europe, USA, Canada, Australia, Japan

Cover: Foto ©Andreas Hilbeck / pixelio.de

More available books at **www.hansebooks.com**

THE ROMANCE OF GOLDEN STAR

Hail, Son of the Sun!

Page 78.

THE ROMANCE OF GOLDEN STAR.
Frontispiece.

THE ROMANCE OF GOLDEN STAR . . .

BY

GEORGE GRIFFITH

AUTHOR OF

'THE ANGEL OF THE REVOLUTION,'
'OLGA ROMANOFF,' 'THE OUTLAWS
OF THE AIR,' 'VALDAR THE OFT-
BORN,' 'BRITON OR BOER?' ETC., ETC.

ILLUSTRATED . .
BY ALFRED PEARSE

*' To that Son of the Sacred Race
who for Honour and Faith and
Love shall take the hand of a
pure virgin of his own holy blood
and with her pass fearless through
the Gate of Death into the shadows
which lie beyond shall be given the
glory of casting out the Oppressor
and raising the Rainbow Banner
once more above the Golden Throne
of the Incas. On that Throne he
shall sit and wield power and mete
out justice and mercy to the Children of the Sun when the gloom
that is falling upon the Land of
the Four Regions shall have passed
away in the dawn of a brighter
age.'*

—THE PROPHECY CONTAINED
IN THE ANCIENT LEGEND
OF VILCAROYA-INCA AND
GOLDEN STAR, HIS SISTER-
BRIDE.

LONDON : F. V. WHITE & CO. . . .
14 BEDFORD STREET, STRAND, W.C. 1897

CONTENTS

CHAPTER VII

LIST OF ILLUSTRATIONS

BY

ALFRED PEARSE

The Romance of Golden Star

PROLOGUE

I

HIS HIGHNESS THE MUMMY

'AH, what a thing it would be for us if his Inca Highness were really only asleep, as he looks to be! Just think what he could tell us—how easily he could re-create that lost wonderland of his for us, what riddles he could answer, what lies he could contradict. And then think of all the lost treasures that he could show us the way to. Upon my word, if Mephistopheles were to walk into this room just now, I think I should be tempted to make a bargain with him. Do you know, Djama, I believe I would give half the remainder of my own life, whatever that may be, to learn the secrets that were once locked up in that withered, desiccated brain of his.'

The speaker was one of two men who were standing in a large room, half-study, half-museum, in a big, old-fashioned house in Maida Vale. Wherever the science of archæology was studied, Professor Martin Lamson was known as the highest living authority on the subject of the antiquities of South America. He had just returned from a year's relic-hunting in Peru and Bolivia, and was enjoying the luxury of unpacking his treasures with the almost boyish delight which, under such circumstances, comes only to the true enthusiast. His companion was a somewhat slenderly-built man, of medium height, whose clear, olive skin, straight, black hair, and deep blue-black eyes betrayed a not very remote Eastern origin.

Dr Laurens Djama was a physiologist, whose rapidly-acquired fame—he was barely thirty-two—would have been considered sounder by his professional brethren if it had not been, as they thought, impaired by excursions into by-ways of science which were believed to lead him perilously near to the borders of occultism. Five years before he had pulled the professor through a very bad attack of the calentura in Panama, where they met by the merest traveller's chance, and since then they had been fast friends.

They were standing over a long packing-case, some seven feet in length and two and a-half in breadth, in which lay, at full length, wrapped in grave-clothes that had once been gaily coloured, but which were now faded and grey with the grave-dust, the figure of a man with hands crossed over the breast, dead to all appearances, and yet so gruesomely lifelike that it seemed hard to believe that the broad, muscular chest over which the crossed hands lay was not actually heaving and falling with the breath of life.

The face had been uncovered. It was that of a man still in the early prime of life. The dull brown hair was long and thick, the features somewhat aquiline, and stamped even in death with an almost royal dignity. The skin was of a pale bronze, though darkened by the hues of death. Yet every detail of the face was so perfect and so life-like, that, as the professor had said, it seemed to be rather the face of a man in a deep sleep than that of an Inca prince who must have been dead and buried for over three hundred years. The closed eyes, though somewhat sunken in their sockets, were the eyes of sleep rather than of death, and the lids seemed to lie so lightly over them that it looked as though one awakening touch would raise them.

'It is beyond all question the most perfect specimen of a mummy that I have seen,' said the doctor, stooping down and drawing his thin, nervous fingers very lightly over the dried skin of the right cheek. 'On my honour, I simply can't believe that His Highness, as you call him, ever really went to the other world by any of the orthodox routes. If you could imagine an absolute suspension of all the vital functions induced by the influence of something—some drug or hypnotic process unknown to modern science, brought into action on a human being in the very prime of his vital strength—then, so far as I can see, the results of that influence would be exactly what you see here.'

'But surely that can't be anything but a dream. How could it be possible to bring all the vital functions to a dead stop like that, and yet keep them in such a state that it might be possible— for that's what I suppose you are driving at—to start them into activity again, just as one might wind up a clock that had been stopped for a few weeks and set it going?'

'My dear fellow, the borderland between life and death is so utterly unknown to the very best of us that there is no telling what frightful possibilities there may be lying hidden under the shadows that hang over it. You know as well as I do that there are perfectly well authenticated instances on record of Hindoo Fakirs who have allowed themselves to be placed in a state of suspended animation and had their tongues turned back into their throats, their mouths and noses covered with clay, and have been buried in graves that have been filled up and had sentries watching day and night over them for as long a period as six weeks, and then have been dug up and restored to perfect health and strength again in a few hours. Now, if life can be suspended for six weeks and then restored to an organism which, from all physiological standpoints, must be regarded as inanimate, why not for six years or six hundred years, for the matter of that? Given once the possibility, which we may assume as proved, of a restoration to life after total suspension of animation, then it only becomes a question of preservation of tissue for more or less indefinite periods. Granted that tissue can be so preserved, then, given the other possibility already proved, and—well, we will talk about the other possibility afterwards. Now, tell me, don't you, as an archæologist, see anything peculiar about this Inca prince of yours?'

The professor had been looking keenly at his friend during the delivery of this curious physiological lecture. He seemed as though he were trying to read the thoughts that were chasing each other through his brain behind the impenetrable mask of that smooth, broad forehead of his. He looked into his eyes, but saw nothing there save a cold, steady light that he had often seen before when the doctor was discussing subjects that interested him deeply. As for his face, it was utterly impassive—the face of a dispassionate scientist quietly discussing the possible solution of a problem that had been laid before him. Whether his friend was really driving at some unheard-of and unearthly solution of the problem which he himself had raised, or whether he was merely discussing the possible issue of some abstract question in physiology, he was utterly unable to discover, and so he thought it best to confine himself to the matter in hand, without hazarding any risky guesses that might possibly result in his own confusion. So he answered as quietly as he could:

'Yes, I must confess that there are two perhaps very important points of difference between this and any other Peruvian mummy that I have ever seen or heard of.'

'Ah, I thought so,' said Djama, half closing his eyes and allowing just the ghost of a smile to flit across his lips. 'I thought I knew enough about archæology. and the science of mummies in general to expect you to say that. Now, just for the gratification of my own vanity, I should like to try and anticipate what you are going to say; and if I'm wrong, well, of course, I shall only be too happy to be contradicted.'

'Very well,' laughed the professor; 'say on!'

'Well, in the first place, I believe I'm right in saying that all Peruvian mummies that have so far been discovered have been found in a sitting posture, with the legs drawn close up to the body by means of bindings and burial-clothes, so that the chin rested between the knees, while the arms were brought round the legs and folded over them. Then, again, these mummies have always been found in an upright position, while you found this one lying down.'

'Quite so, quite so!' said the professor. 'In fact, I may say that no one save myself has ever discovered such a mummy as this among all the thousands that have been taken out of Peruvian burying-places. And now, what is your other point?'

'Simply this,' said Djama, kneeling down beside the case, and laying his hands over the abdomen of the recumbent figure. 'In the case of all mummies, whether Egyptian or Peruvian, it was the invariable practice of the embalmers to take out the intestines and fill the abdominal cavity with preservative herbs and spices. Now, this has not been done in this case. Look here.'

And deftly and swiftly he moved the dusty, half-decayed coverings from the body of the mummy, while the professor looked on half-wondering and half-frightened for the safety of his treasure.

'That has not been done here. You see the man's body is as perfect as it was on the day he died—to use a conventional term. Now, am I not right?'

'Yes, yes; perfectly right,' answered the professor, who felt himself fast losing his grip of the conversation which had taken so strange a turn. 'But what has all this got to do with the most unique mummy that ever was brought from South America? Surely, in the name of all that's sacred, you don't mean—'

'My dear fellow, never mind what I mean for the present,' replied Djama, with another of his half smiles. 'If I mean anything at all, the meaning will keep, and if I don't it doesn't matter. Now, do you mind telling me exactly how and where you came across this extraordinary specimen of—well, for want of a better term—we will say, Inca embalming?'

'Yes, willingly,' said the professor, glad to get back again on to the familiar ground of his own experiences. 'I found it almost by accident in a little valley about four days' ride to the westward of Cuzco. I was on my way to Abancay across the Apurimac. My mule had fallen lame, and so I got belated. Night came on, and somehow we got off the track crossing one of the Punas—those elevated tablelands, you know, up among the mountains—and when the mule could go no farther we camped, and the next morning I found myself in an almost circular valley, completely walled in by enormous mountains, save for the narrow, crooked gorge through which we had stumbled by the purest accident. The bottom of this valley was filled by a little lake, and while I was exploring the shores of this I saw, hidden underneath an overhanging ledge of rock, a couple of courses of that wonderful mortarless masonry which the Incas alone seemed to know how to build. I had no sooner seen it than all desire of getting to Abancay or anywhere else had left me. I made my arriero turn the animals loose for the day, and then I sent him back to a village we had passed through the day before to buy more provisions and bring them to me.

'As soon as he had got out of sight I set to work to get some of the stones out and see what there was behind them. I knew there must be something, for the Incas never wasted labour. It was hard work, for the stones were fitted together as perfectly as the pieces of a Chinese puzzle; but at last I got one out and then the rest was easy. Behind the stones I found a little chamber hollowed out of the rock, perfectly clean and dry, and on the floor of this I found, without any other covering than what you see there, the mummy of His Highness lying on what had once been a bed of soft Vicuña skins, as perfect and as lifelike as though he had only crept in there twelve hours before, and had laid down for a good night's rest.

'You may imagine how delighted I was at such

a find. I hardly knew how to contain myself until my man came back. I put the stones back into their places as well as I could, and when Patricio returned the next day I had the animals saddled up, and started off in a hurry to Cuzco. There I had this case made, bought two extra mules, brought them to the valley, packed up my mummy, took it back to Cuzco, and from there to the railway terminus at Sicuani and took it down by train to Arequipa, where I left it in safe keeping until I had finished the rest of my exploration. Then I went back, took it down to Mollendo, got it on board the steamer, and here it is.'

' And you didn't find any traces of other treasure-places, I suppose, in the valley?' said Djama, who had listened with the most perfect attention to the professor's story.

'No, I didn't, though I must confess that one side of the cave in which I found this was walled up with the same kind of masonry as there was in front of it; but, to tell you the truth, the Peruvian Government has such insane ideas about treasure-hunting; and the life of a man who is believed to have discovered anything worth stealing is worth so little in the wilder districts of the interior, that I was afraid of losing the treasure I had got, perhaps for the sake of a few little gold ornaments which I might have dug out of the hill, and so I decided to be content with what I'd found.'

'H'm!' said the doctor. 'Well, you may have been wise under the circumstances; I daresay you were. But we can see about that afterwards Meanwhile there is something else to be talked about.'

He stopped suddenly, took a quick turn or two up and down the room, with his hands clasped behind him and his eyes fixed on the floor. Then he went to the door, opened it, looked out, shut it and locked it, and then came back again and sat down without a word in his chair, staring steadily at the impassive face of the mummy in the packing-case.

'Why, what's the matter, doctor?' said the professor, a trifle sharply. 'You don't suppose I am afraid of anyone coming to steal my treasure, do you?'

'My dear fellow,' said Djama, looking him straight in the eyes, and speaking very slowly, as though his mind was doing something else besides shaping the thoughts to which he was giving utterance, 'I don't for a moment suppose that there are thieves about, or that, if there were, any burglar with a competent knowledge of his profession would think of stealing your mummy, priceless as it may prove to be. I locked the door because I don't want to be interrupted.

I want to talk to you about a very important matter.'

'And that is?'

'Mephistopheles.'

'WHAT?'

'Gently, my friend, gently, don't get excited yet. You will want all your nerves soon, I can assure you. Yes, I am quite serious. You know that in the good old days, when people still believed in His Majesty of Darkness, such a speech as the one you remember making a short time ago was quite enough to call up one of his agents, armed with full powers to make contracts and do all necessary business.'

'Look here, Laurens, if you go on talking like that, I shall begin to think you have gone out of your mind.'

'My dear fellow, to be quite candid with you, I don't care two pins what you think on that subject. I have been called mad too many times for that. Now, suppose, just for argument's sake, that I were Mephistopheles, and staked my diabolic reputation on the statement that in that thing you possess a possible key to those lost treasures of the Incas, which ten generations of men have hunted for in vain, what kind of a bargain would you be inclined to make with me on the strength of it? Half the rest of your life, I think you said, and as that wouldn't be very much good to me, suppose we say the half of any treasures we may discover by the help of our silent friend there?   Eh?—will that suit you?'

'Are you really serious, Djama, or are you only dreaming another of these wild scientific dreams of yours?' exclaimed the professor, taking a couple of quick strides towards him. 'What connection can there possibly be between a mummy, about four centuries years old, and the lost treasures of the Incas?'

'This man was an Inca, wasn't he?' said the doctor, abruptly, ' and one of the highest rank, too, from what you have said. He lived just about the time of the Conquest, didn't he—the time when the priests stripped their temples, and the nobles emptied their palaces of their treasures to save them from the Spaniards? Is it not likely that he would know where, at anyrate, a great part of them was buried? Nay, may he not even have known the localities of the lost mines that the Incas got their hundredweights of gold from, and of the emerald mines which no one has ever been able to find? Why, Lamson, if these dead lips could speak, I believe they could make you and me millionaires in an hour. And why shouldn't they speak?'

'Don't talk like that, Djama, for Heaven's sake! It is too serious a thing to joke about,' said the professor, with a half-frightened glance in his set and shining eyes. 'I should have thought you, of all men, knew enough of the facts of life and death not to talk such nonsense as that.'

'Nonsense!' said the physiologist, interrupting him almost angrily; 'may I not know enough of the facts of life and death, as you call them, to know that that is *not* nonsense? But there, it's no use arguing about things like this. Will you allow this mummy of yours to be made the subject of—well, we will say, an experiment in physiology?'

'What! the finest and most unique huaca that was ever brought to Europe—'

'It would only be made finer still by the experiment, even if it failed. I know what you are going to say, and I will give you my word of honour, and, if you like, I'll pledge you my professional reputation, that not a hair of its head shall be injured. Let me take it to my laboratory, and I promise you solemnly that in a week you shall have it back, not as it is now, but either the body of your Inca, as perfect as it was the day he died, or—'

He stopped, and looked hard at his friend, as if wondering what the effects of his next words would be upon him.

'Or what?' asked the professor, almost in a whisper.

'Your Inca prince, roused from his three-hundred-year sleep, and able to answer your questions and guide us to his lost mines and treasure houses.'

'Are you in earnest, Djama?' the professor whispered, catching him by the arm and looking round at the mummy as though he half thought that the silent witness in the packing-case might be listening to the words which, if it could have heard, would have had such a terrible significance for it. 'Do you really mean to say in sober earnest that there is the remotest chance of your science being able to work such a miracle as that?'

'A chance, yes,' replied Djama, steadily. 'It is not a certainty, of course, but I believe it to be possible. Will you let me try?'

'Yes, you shall try,' answered the professor in a voice nothing like as steady as his. 'If any other man but you had even hinted at such a thing, I would have seen him—well, in a lunatic asylum first. But there, I will trust my Inca to you. It seems a fearful thing even to attempt, and yet, after all, if it fails there will be no harm done, and if it succeeds—ah, yes, if it succeeds—it will mean—'

'Endless fame for you, my friend, as the re-creator of a lost society, and for both of us wealth, perhaps beyond counting. But stop a moment—granted success, how shall we talk with our Inca *revenant?* Have I not heard you say that the

Aymaru dialect of the Quichua tongue is lost as completely as the Inca treasures?'

'Not quite, though I believe I am now the only white man on earth who understands it.'

'Good! then let me get to work at once, and in a week—well, in a week we shall see.'

II

A PHYSIOLOGICAL EXPERIMENT

LAURENS DJAMA dined with the professor that night, and the small hours were growing large before they ended the long talk of which their strange bargain, and the still stranger experiment which was to result from it, formed the subject. The next day the packing-case containing the mummy was transferred to Djama's laboratory, and then for a whole week neither the professor nor any of his friends or acquaintances had either sight or speech of him.

Every caller at his house in Brondesbury Park was politely but firmly denied admittance on professional grounds, and three letters and two telegrams which the professor had sent to him, after being himself denied admittance, remained unanswered.

At last, on the Thursday following the Friday on which the mummy had been sent to the laboratory, the professor received a telegram telling him to come at once to the doctor. Three minutes after he had read it he was in a hansom and on his way to Kilburn, wondering what it was that he was to be brought face to face with during the next half hour.

This time there was no denial. The door opened as he went up the steps, and the servant handed him a note. He tore it open and read,—

'Come round to the laboratory and make a new acquaintance who will yet be an old one.'

His heart stood still, and he caught his breath sharply as he read the words which told him that the unearthly experiment for which he had furnished the subject had been successful.

The doctor's laboratory stood apart from the house in the long, narrow garden at the back, and as he approached the door he stopped for a moment, and an almost irresistible impulse to go away and have nothing more to do with the unholy work in hand took possession of him. Then the love of his science and the longing to hear the marvels which could only be heard from the lips that had been silent for centuries overcame his fears, and he went up to the door and knocked softly.

It was opened by a haggard, wild-eyed man, whom he scarcely recognised as his old friend.

Djama did not speak; he simply caught hold of the sleeve of his coat with a nervous, trembling grasp, drew him in, shut the door, and led him to a corner of the room where there was a little camp bed, curtained all round with thin, transparent muslin, through which he could see the shape of a man lying under the sheets.

Djama pulled the curtain aside, and said in a hoarse whisper,—

'Look, it has been hard work, and terrible work, too, but I have succeeded. Do you see, he is breathing!'

The professor stared wide-eyed at the white pillow on which lay the head of what, a week before, had been his mummy. Now it was the head of a living man; the pale bronze of the skin was clear and moist with the dew of life; the lips were no longer brown and dry, but faintly red and slightly parted, and the counterpane, which was pulled close up under the chin, was slowly rising and falling with the regular rhythm of a sleeper's breathing. He looked from the face of him who had been dead and was alive again to the face of the man whose daring science and perfect skill had wrought the unholy miracle, and then he shrank back from the bedside, pulling Djama with him, and whispering,—

Good God, it is even more awful than it is wonderful! How did you do it?'

'That is my secret,' whispered Djama, his dry lips shaping themselves into a ghastly smile, 'and for all the treasures that that man ever saw, I wouldn't tell it to a living soul, or do such hideous work again. I tell you I have seen life and death fighting together for two days and nights in this room—not, mind you, as they fight on a death-bed, but the other way, and I would rather see a thousand men die than one more come back out of death into life. You see, he is sleeping now. He opened his eyes just before daybreak this morning—that's nearly ten hours ago—but if I lived ten thousand years I should never forget that one look he gave me before he shut them again. Since then he has slept, and I stood by that bed testing his pulse and his breathing for eight hours before I wired you. Then I knew he would live, and so I sent for you.'

The professor looked at his friend with an involuntary and unconquerable aversion rising in his heart against him ; an aversion that was half fear, half horror, and then he remembered that he himself had a share in the fearful work which had been done—a work that could not now be undone without murder.

With another backward look at the bed, he said, in a whisper that was almost a smothered groan,—

'When will he wake ?'

Before Djama could reply, the question was answered by a faint rustle, and a low, long-drawn sigh from the bed. They looked and saw the Inca's face turned towards them, and two fever-bright eyes shining through the curtains.

'He is awake already, two hours sooner than I expected,' said Djama, in a voice that he strove vainly to keep steady. 'Come, now, you are the only man on earth who can talk to him. Let us see if he has come back to reason as well as to life.'

'Yes, I will try,' said the professor, faintly. He took a couple of trembling steps. Then the lights in the room began to dance, the whitewashed walls reeled round him, and he pitched forward and fell unconscious by the side of the bed.

When he came to himself he was lying on the floor of the laboratory, out of sight of the bed, behind a great cupboard, glass-doored and filled with bottles. Djama was kneeling beside him. A strong smell of ammonia dominated the other smells peculiar to a laboratory, and his brow was wet with the spirit that Djama was gently rubbing on it with his hand.

'What have I been doing?' he said, as, with the other's assistance, he got up into a sitting position and looked stupidly about him. 'It isn't true, that is it, I really saw—Good God no, it can't be; it's too horrible. I must have dreamt it.'

'Nonsense, my dear fellow, nonsense! I should have thought you would have had better nerves than that. Come, take a nip of this, and pull yourself together. There is nothing so very horrible about it for you. Now, if you had had the actual work to do—'

'Then it *is* true! You really have brought him back to life again? That was him I saw lying on the bed?' He looked up at Djama as he spoke with a half-inquiring, half-frightened glance. His voice was weak and unsteady, like the voice of a man who has been stunned by some terrible shock, and is still dazed with the fear and wonder of it.

'Yes, of course it was,' said Djama; 'but I can tell you, I should have hesitated before I introduced you so suddenly, if I hadn't thought that the nerves of an old traveller like you would have been a good deal stronger than they seem to be. It's a very good job that His Highness was only about half conscious himself when you collapsed, or you might have given him a shock that would have killed him again.'

'Again?' said the professor, echoing the last word as he got up slowly to his feet. 'That sounds queer, doesn't it, to talk of killing a man *again?* I am more sorry than I can say that I was weak enough to let my feelings overcome me in such a ridiculous fashion. However, I am all right now. Give me another drain of that brandy of yours, and then let us talk. Is he still awake?'

'No, he dozed off again almost immediately, and you have been here about ten minutes or a quarter of an hour. Do you think you can stand another look at him?'

'Oh, certainly,' said the professor, who, as a matter of· fact, felt a trifle ashamed of himself and his weakness, and was anxious to do something that would restore his credit. He followed the doctor out into the laboratory again, and stood with him for some moments without speaking by the Inca's bedside. He was sleeping very quietly, and his breathing seemed to be stronger and deeper than it had been. He had slightly shifted his position, and was lying now half turned on his right side, with his right cheek on the pillow.

'You see he has moved,' whispered Djama. 'That shows that muscular control has been re-established. We shall have him walking about in a day or so. Ah! he is dreaming, and of something pleasant, too. Look at his lips moving into a smile. Poor fellow, just fancy a man dreaming of things that happened three hundred years ago, and waking up to find himself in another world. I'll be bound he is dreaming about his wife or sweetheart, and we shall have to tell him, or rather you will, that she has been a mummy for three centuries. Look now, his lips are moving; I believe he is going to say something. See if you can hear what it is?'

The professor stooped down and held his ear so close that he could feel on his cheek the gentle fanning of the breath that had been still for three centuries. Then the Inca's lips moved again, and a soft sighing sound came from them, and in the midst of it he caught the words,—

'*Cori-Coyllur, Ñustallipa, Ñusta mi!*'

Then there came a long, gentle sigh. The Inca's lips became still again, shaped into a very sweet and almost womanly smile, as though his vision had passed and left him in a happy, dreamless slumber.

'What did he say?' whispered Djama. 'Were you able to understand it?'

'Yes,' said the professor, 'yes, and you were right about the subject of his dream. Come away, in case we wake him, and I will tell you.'

They went to the other end of the laboratory, and the professor went on, still speaking in a low, half-whisper,—

'Poor fellow, I am afraid we have incurred a terribly heavy debt to him. What he said meant, "Golden Star, my princess, my darling!" So you see you were right, but poor Golden Star has been dead three hundred years and more—that is, at least, if his Golden Star is the same as the heroine of the tradition.'

'What tradition?' asked Djama.

'It's too long a story to tell you now, but if she is the same, then our Inca's name is Vilcaroya, and he is the hero of the strangest story, and, thanks to you, the strangest fate that the wildest romancer could imagine. However, the story must keep, for I wouldn't spoil it by cutting it short. The principal question now is—what are we going to do with him? We can't keep him here, of course?'

'No, certainly not,' replied Djama, with knitted brows and faintly smiling lips. 'His Highness must be cared for in accordance with his rank and our expectations. I shall have him taken into the house and properly nursed.'

'But what about your sister? You will frighten her to death if you take in a living patient that has been dead for three hundred years.'

'Not if we manage it properly; there will be no need to tell Ruth the story yet, at anyrate. I'll tell her that I am going to receive a patient who is suffering from a mysterious disease unknown

to medical science. I'll say I picked him up in
the Oriental Home in Whitechapel, and have
brought him here to study him, and you and
I must smuggle him into the house and put
him to bed some time when she is out of the way.
Then I'll instal her as nurse; in fact, she will do
that for herself; and as there is no chance of her
learning anything from him, we can break the
truth to her by degrees, and when His Highness
is well enough to travel we'll all be off to Peru
and come back millionaires, if you can only persuade him to tell you the secret of his treasure-
houses.'

That night the doctor and the professor took
turns in watching by the bedside of their strange
patient, whose slumber became lighter and lighter
until, towards midnight, he got so restless and
apparently uneasy that Djama considered that
the time had come to wake him and see if he
was able to take any nourishment. So he set
the professor to work, warming some chicken
broth over a spirit lamp, and mixing a little
champagne and soda - water in one glass and
brandy and water in another. Meanwhile, he
filled a hypodermic syringe with colourless fluid
out of a little stoppered bottle, and then turned
the sheet down and injected the contents of the
syringe under the smooth, bronze skin of the
Inca's shoulder. He moved slightly at the prick

of the needle, then he drew two or three deep breaths, and suddenly sat up in bed and stared about him with wide open eyes, full, as they well might be, of inquiring wonder.

The professor, who had turned at the sound of the hurried breathing, saw him as he raised himself, and heard him say in the clear and somewhat high-pitched tone of a dweller among the mountains,—

'Has the morning dawned again for the Children of the Sun? Am I truly awake, or am I only dreaming that the death-sleep is over? Where is Golden Star, and where am I? Tell me—you who have doubtless brought me back to the life we forsook together—was it last night or how many nights or moons ago?'

The words came slowly at first, like those of a man still on the borderland between sleep and waking; but each one was spoken more clearly and decisively than the one before it, and the last sentence was uttered in the strong, steady tones of a man in full possession of his faculties.

'Come here, Lamson,' said Djama, a trifle nervously; 'bring the soup with you, and some brandy, though I don't think he needs it. Do you understand what he said?'

'Yes,' replied the professor, coming to the bedside with a cup of soup in one hand and a glass of brandy and water in the other. Both hands

"Am I only dreaming that the death-sleep is over?"

To face page 26.

trembled as he set the cup and the glass down on a little table. He looked at the Inca like a man looking at a re-embodied spirit, and said to him in Quichua,—

'I am not he who has brought you back to life, but my friend here, who is a great and skilled physician, and master of the arts of life and death. You are in his house, and safe, for we are friends, and have nursed you back to health and waking life after your long sleep.'

'But Golden Star,' said the Inca, interrupting him with a flash of impatience in his eyes. 'Where is she — my bride who went with me into the shades of death? Have you not brought her, too, back to life?'

The professor stared in silence at the strange speaker of these strange words, which told him so plainly that the old legend of the death-bridal of Vilcaroya-Inca and Golden Star was now no legend at all, but a true story which had come down almost unchanged from generation to generation. Then an infinite pity filled his heart for this lonely wanderer from another age, whose friends and kindred had been dead for centuries, and whose very nation was now only a shadowy name on a half-forgotten page of history.

'What does he say?' said Djama, breaking in upon his reverie. 'I suppose he wants to know where he is, and what has become of that sweet-heart of his he was dreaming about?'

'Yes,' replied the professor; 'but you won't understand properly until I have told you the story. Poor fellow! I suppose we shall have to tell him the ghastly truth. Good Heavens! fancy telling a man that his wife has been dead for three hundred years or more! Look here, Djama, this business can't stop here, you know. What a fool I was, after all, not to see if there wasn't another chamber beside the one I found him in! Of course there must be, and I have no doubt she is lying there at this present moment. We shall have to go and find her, and you must restore her as you have done him. Phew! where is it all going to end, I wonder!'

'And suppose we can't find her, or suppose I fail, even if I can bring myself to undertake that horrible work all over again?' said Djama, looking almost fearfully at the Inca, who was still sitting up in the bed glancing mutely from one to the other, as though waiting for an answer to his question. Then, keeping his voice as steady as he could, the professor told him the story of his resuscitation, addressing him by his own name and ending by asking him if he remembered when he and Golden Star had devoted them-selves to die together, as the tradition said they had done.

'Yes, I remember!' said Vilcaroya, with brightening eyes and faintly flushing cheeks. 'How could I forget it? It was when the bearded strangers from the north had come and taken the usurper Atahuallpa prisoner in the midst of his conquering host at Cajamarca. It was after the Inca Huascar had been slain by stealth with a traitor's knife. It was on the night of the feast of Raymi, when our Father the Sun had left the Sacred Fleece unkindled, and when was fulfilled the prophecy that the night should fall over the land of the Children of the Sun. Now, tell me, you who speak the language of my people, how long have I been sleeping?'

Instead of replying directly, he offered the Inca the cup of broth, and asked him first to take the nourishment that he must need so greatly after his long fast, telling him that it was needful to prevent him losing his new-found strength again. When he had eaten and drunk a little, then he would tell him what he could.

He took the broth and a little bread obediently, and while he was eating and drinking, the professor translated what he had said to the doctor. When he had finished, Djama looked at the Inca, sitting there taking food and drink like any other human being, and with evident relish, too, and said,—

'That happened in 1532—three hundred and

sixty-five years ago! It sounds utterly incredible, doesn't it, and yet there he is, eating and drinking and talking with us just like any other man. I can hardly believe the work of my own hands, and I am beginning to half wish I had never begun it. Just imagine the awful loneliness to which we shall have condemned this poor fellow, supposing we can't find his Golden Star and re-store her to him! Still perhaps you had better tell him the truth at once. I think he can stand it. He has been a long time coming round, but I don't think there is much the matter with him now.'

Then the professor told Vilcaroya the, to him, so terrible truth, that of all men in the world he was the most lonely, separated as he was from all that he had known and loved by an impassable gulf of nearly four long centuries—that his well-loved Golden Star was but a memory known to few, a name in a vague tradition ; that the resting-place, even of her mummy, was unknown, and that all that the darkest prophecy could have foretold had in very truth fallen upon the land of the Incas and the Children of the Sun.

Vilcaroya heard him to the end in silence; then, raising his hands to his forehead, he bowed his head and said,—

' It is the will of our Father, foretold by the lips of his priests, but other things were foretold which shall be fulfilled as well as these. Golden Star is not dead; she only sleeps as I did. If I have awakened, why shall not she? I know where she lies—where Anda-Huillac swore to me they would lay her. Come, let us go! I will take you to the place, and you shall restore her to me, warm and living and loving as she was when I kissed her good-bye in the Sanctuary of the Sun, and I will give you treasures of gold and silver and jewels such as you have never dreamed of in exchange for her.'

THE STORY OF VILCAROYA

CHAPTER I

BACK THROUGH THE SHADOWS

As the time passes between dreaming and waking, so for me did the long years pass, flowing like a smooth and silent stream seen from afar, out of the darkness that fell so slowly and so sweetly over my eyes that night when I sank into the death-trance beside Golden Star, my beloved, in the bridal chamber that they made for us in the Temple of the Sun, into the light that shone into them when they opened upon a scene so different, and saw a white, haggard face bending over me, and two black, burning eyes looking into them.

Then I closed them again and slept, and when I woke again there were two faces looking at me, both white and full of fear and wonder, and I saw two beings who seemed very strange to me, such as I had never seen among the Children of the

Sun, standing by the couch on which I lay, and one of them fell down as though sore stricken, and I tried to think what this could mean, and, thinking, fell asleep again.

Then I dreamt a long, sweet dream of the days that I now know were far past, when I, Vilcaroya, son of the great Huayna-Capac, lived in the Land of the Four Regions, a prince among princes, a warrior and a child of the Sacred Race, whose blood had flowed unmixed through many generations from the divine fountain of life and light, our Father the Sun. I dreamt of Golden Star, and the days when I loved her in timid silence, for she was the fairest of all our race, and so, as it seemed to me, destined to no less a lot than the motherhood of a long line of Incas, in whom should live and grow to ever greater splendour the glories of the race that owned no earthly origin.

I called her in my dream, but she made no answer. I saw her lying by my side in that well-remembered chamber, with the shadowy forms of the priests standing about us as I had seen them long before; but, alas! she lay still with closed eyes and lips which seemed to have forgotten how sweetly they once could smile. I whispered her name, mingled with many a loving word, into her ear, and still she moved not. I put my arms about her and kissed her, and instantly I shrank back shivering with a fear unspeakable, for the form

C

that should have been so warm and soft and yielding, was chilled and pulseless and rigid, as though some foul magic had changed it into stone, and the lips that should have given me back kiss for kiss were still and cold and senseless.

Then I saw, as it seemed with half-closed eyes, that dear shape of hers being borne away from me, while I, longing to snatch her from the hands of those who were robbing me of her, yet lay helpless on the couch, without strength to move or speak, until all grew dim around me, and I felt myself raised by invisible hands, and borne far away through the darkness—and so my dream melted away into the night of sleep.

Then, yet again, I woke and saw the two strange men that I had seen before, and one came and spoke to me kindly in my own tongue, and called me by my own name, and gave me food and drink, and told me in a few, but to me terrible, words that the dreams I had dreamed were dreams indeed—dreams of a time that was long gone by, of things that had passed away, perchance for ever, and men and women whose names were only memories.

Thus did I come from the evening of one age into the morning of another, falling asleep in the prime of my strength and manhood, and waking again even as I had fallen asleep—though those who had closed my eyes had been dead for many generations, and the name of our ancient race was but a bitter memory to the sons and daughters of my own land amidst the mountains.

Then I went forth into the wondrous new world into which I had awakened, the world which you who read this hold so common, and which I found crowded with wonders so many and marvellous that if it had not been for the loving care of her who guided my first footsteps on my new journey, as she might have guided those of a little child, my re-awakening reason must soon have been quenched in the night of madness.

Many and strange as were the things that happened to me during the first days and months of my awakening, there is little need that I should now write of them at any length. Yet something I must say of them in order that the still stranger things of which I shall have to tell may be the better understood.

And first I must tell of her whose gentle hand led me from weakness to strength, and guided my unwonted footsteps through the mazes of that new wonderland in which I had awakened, and from whose lips I learnt the first words that I spoke of the strong and stately English speech in which I am striving so lamely and imperfectly to write down the story of my new life.

This was Ruth, the sister of Djama, whose

smile was the first ray of sunshine that shone into my second life, and whose laugh was so sweet and gladsome, that when it first sounded in my ears, like an echo from the dear dead past, I named her forthwith Cusi-Coyllur, which in English means Joyful Star—after that royal maiden of my own race who loved the handsome rebel Ollantay, and, refusing all others, waited for him in the House of the Virgins of the Sun until he came in triumph to claim her. She came with us to the south, rejecting all contrary counsel and braving the labours of the long, toilsome journey, so that she might be the first woman to welcome Golden Star back into the world of life.

Yet what words can I find in this new speech that I have yet but half learnt to tell fitly of her beauty and sweet graciousness, and of all the magic which made her seem in my eyes like an angel that had come down from the Mansions of the Sun to greet me in a world in which I was a stranger? Better that you who may read what I write should learn to know her for yourself through the sweetness and grace of her own words and deeds, as I shall strive, however unworthily, to tell of them. So, then, let it be.

But there is another of whom I must say something before I go on to tell of my return to my own land—now, alas! mine no longer—and that is Francis Hartness, a captain among the warriors of the English, and a friend of him who was called the professor, because of his learning —he who had helped Djama to bring me back into the world of living men.

He was a man of about thirty years, tall of stature and strong of limb, brief of speech and straight of tongue, with eyes as blue as the skies which shine on Yucay, and hair and beard golden and bright as the rays which flow from the smile of our Father the Sun. Him we met by chance one evening in the square of the town which is called Panama, named, they told me, after that older city, whence the conquerors of my people sailed to ravish the realms of Huayna-Capac. There was peace in his own land and all the neighbouring countries, and so he was journeying to the region which is now called South America, where the descendants of the Spaniards are nearly always fighting among themselves over the spoils of my people, to see what work he could find to keep his sword from rusting.

As he was greatly skilled in that strange, new warfare of flame and thunder and far-smiting bolts, which had but begun to be when our Father the Sun hid his face from the eyes of his children, I took counsel with Joyful Star— who was ever my wisest as well as my most faithful guide in all things — and we together told him my story as we went south, and after that I had asked him if he would help me in the task which I was going to essay, which was nothing less than the taking back of the land of my fathers, and the raising of the children of my people to the ancient glories of that state which I alone of living men remembered. To this, after some shrewd questioning, he consented —for it was a desperate venture, such as his brave heart loved—and when he had given me his hand on it, and promised, after the simple fashion of his nation, to be true to me in peace and war, I told him of the means that I could employ to gain my end, and how I would use that lust of gold which had led to the ruin of my people, so that it should conquer the children of their conquerors and give me back the empire that had been my father's.

At Panama we took ship again and travelled swiftly and straightly south, driven by that wondrous power which had come into the world to serve men like a tireless giant since I had fallen asleep; and day after day on the southward voyage I walked alone up and down the deck, or stood gazing, rapt in thought, at the desert foreshore along which the steamer was running, and at the great masses of the dark brown barren mountains, as they towered range beyond range till they overtopped the clouds themselves and stood serene and sharply outlined against the blue background of the upper sky.

Behind those mighty, rock-built ramparts lay the well-loved, well-remembered land over which my fathers had ruled in the days of peace, before the stranger and the oppressor had come. On the other side of them I knew that I was now fated to find only the poor fragments of the great cities and stately pleasure-houses that I had known in all their strength and beauty— only the silent and deserted ruins of the mighty fortresses which had guarded the confines of our lost empire, and were the portals through which the Children of the Sun had marched to unvarying conquest.

I thought, too, of the broad, green, level plain of Cajamarca, surrounded by its guardian ramparts of terraced hills; of the long, verdant valley of Cuzco with its hundred towns and villages nestling amidst the foliage which shaded their streets and squares, and looking out over the level fields of the valley and the countless tiers of terraces that rose green and gold with maize, or glowing with flowers, to the summits of the hills; and of that earthly paradise of Yucay, wherein the Gardens of the Sun, the golden shrines of my ancient faith, and the wondrous pleasure-palaces of many generations of Incas had glowed in almost heavenly beauty, embosomed in green and gold and scarlet in the midst of inaccessible mountains which themselves were overtopped by the mighty peaks of eternal snow that I had so often seen glimmering white and ghostly in the moonlight, like guardian spirits round an enchanted realm, on many a night of delicious revelry now far past and lost in the swift flood of the years that had rolled by since then.

It was to the poor remnants of all these glories that I was returning—returning to find, as they had told me, the homes of my ancestors laid waste and the descendants of my people the slaves of strangers. The desolation which it had taken centuries to accomplish would be to me but the swift, magical change of a day and a night and a morning.

Think, you who read, of the dread and the horror of it! I had seen the last day of the stately empire of my fathers the Incas! I had fallen asleep and I had awakened, and now, on the morrow of my sleep, I was coming back to the silent and ghastly ruins which the slow, pitiless work of the years and centuries had left behind it!

But over the gulf of these same centuries the hand of my Father the Sun was swiftly stretched out to help and uphold me, for no sooner did I again tread that soil which had once been sacred to Him, than my fainting heart grew strong with the memory of that ancient prophecy which I had come to fulfil, and of which this new life of mine was of itself a part fulfilment. If one part, and that not the least, had already been made good, then why not the rest?

Far away behind those towering tiers of mountains lay Golden Star in that resting-place to which she had been borne with me, sleeping soundly in the impassive embrace of their mighty arms; and within the safe-keeping of those arms lay, too, that uncounted treasure, that vast legacy which the long-dead leaders of my people had bequeathed to me for the sacred purpose of re-storing those glories which all men, save myself, believed to be but a dream of the distant past, that incomparable inheritance of which I was the sole lawful heir on earth, and which I was coming to share with Golden Star when I had once more raised the Rainbow Banner above the restored throne of the divine Manco.

As I thought of all this, the blood that had lain stagnant through the long years of my magical death-sleep began to pulse like living fire through my veins. My new life with all its marvels became glorified into a waking vision of new conquests and re-won empire. The past was a dream both sweet and bitter in its vivid memories, but still a dream that had been dreamt and was done with. The present and the future were realities, golden and glorious with a hope justified by the miracle that had made them possible. I had learnt enough of the new age in which I had awakened to know that the lust of gold which had brought the conqueror and the oppressor into the land of the Children of the Sun burnt every whit as fiercely in the hearts of the men who were living now as it had done in theirs, and that lust, as I had told Hartness and the others, should now work for me and for the redemption of my people so that that which had been their ruin should yet prove their salvation.

Thus, through the long sunny days and cool, starlit nights did I, Vilcaroya, last of the Incas, muse and dream until I once more stood in the Land of the Four Regions, hale and strong, and burning with the ardour of my sacred mission, ready to dare and do all things, and to use without ruth or scruple that dread power which would so soon lie within my hands to fulfil my oath and Golden Star's, and to accomplish the work that I had come through the shadows of death to do.

So I came back to the shores of that well-loved land of mine which, by the reckoning of the new time into which I had come, had been for more than three hundred years the sport and prey of the generations of strangers and oppressors who had followed those first conquerors of the Children

of the Sun, whose coming had sounded the hour
of doom and ruin through the length and breadth
of that glorious land of green plains and verdant
valleys, of terraced hills and towering mountains,
which had once been our empire and our home.

From the mean coast town of wooden houses
where the railway begins we travelled ever upward
over great, grey, sloping deserts, and by rugged
ravines with steep, broken walls of red earth
and ragged rock; through range after range of
mountains that were all strange and hateful to
me, until we swung round the shoulder of a great
crag-crowned mountain, and I saw across a vast
plain, into which range after range of lesser hills
sloped down, the crystal-white peaks of the snow-
mountains towering far beyond the clouds into the
blue sky above them.

Then I knew that I was coming nearer to the
land that had once been mine, and ere many hours
had passed we stopped in a great city which still
bore its old name of Arequipa, the Place of Rest,
which my own ancestors had given to it. It was
no longer the place of palaces and pleasure-houses,
of flowery gardens and leafy woods that I had
seen it, but above it still gleamed the white snow-
fields and shining peaks of Charchani and Pichu-
Pichu, and between the two great white ranges
still towered the vast, black, snow-crowned cone
of Misti, the smoke-mountain, rising sheer in its

lonely grandeur twelve thousand feet above the sloping plain on which the city lay.

As I looked at it again for the first time after so many years, I asked the professor, as we all called him, if, since I had been asleep, the mountain had been rent asunder again as it had been in the olden times, long before the Spaniards came to seek gold and blood in the Land of the Four Regions. He was very learned in such matters, even as Djama, his friend, was learned in secrets of life and death, and when he told me that the fires within it had slept for more years than men could remember, I was glad. Yet I said nothing of my inward joy, for had I told them all that I knew about the valley of black sand and yellow rock that was hidden behind the far-off wall of snow which shone so whitely against the blue of the midway heaven, it might have been many a long day before we had again set out on our journey towards the place that was the goal at once of my hopes and fears.

We stayed seven days in Arequipa, making our last preparations for the work that lay before us and then we went on again by train to Sicuani, in the valley of the Vilcañota. Then from Sicuani we journeyed on by road, riding on mules through a land that was lovely even in my eyes, though its loveliness was to me only the beauty of ruin and decay, for this was the heart and centre of that vanished empire whose glories no living eyes but mine had ever seen.

I saw wildernesses where there had been gardens, and gaunt, treeless mountains lying bare to the glare of the sun. Lakes that had shone encircled with gardens now spread out dull and stagnant over the neglected fields. A few ragged fragments of grey clay walls still rose from the green plain of Cacha, where I had last seen, in all its glory of gold and rainbow colours, the holy Temple of Viracocha; and the great guardian fortress of Piquillacta, which I had seen stretching its impregnable length and rearing its unscalable height from mountain to mountain across the entrance to the once lovely valley of Cuzco, lay, a huge ragged mass of towering ruins, splendid even in decay.

As we passed through the one half-choked portal that still lay open, I thought, with heavy heart and bowed-down head, of the great fortress as I had seen it in the glory of its pride and strength, of the gallant warriors that had defended it, and the gay processions that I had seen winding in and out of its stately gates, making its hoary walls ring with songs and laughter, and, farther on, as we rode along the valley on that sad and yet eager three days' march of ours, I saw, on the hill-spurs about me, the black and ragged ruins of the fair cities and stately temples and palaces that I had seen crowded with happy throngs, bright with gold and colours, and so fair and strong that no man could have dreamed of the ruin the oppressor had brought upon them.

And so, journeying amidst all these sad memories through a land which, for me, was peopled with the ghosts of my long-dead friends and kindred, we came out at length on the broad, green Plain of the Oracle, and there before me, still nestling under her guardian hills, lay, glimmering white and grey under the slant-ing sun-rays, all that was left of what had once been Cuzco, the City of the Sun and the home of his children. Then, as I lifted my eyes and gazed upon it through the rising mist of my tears, I bowed my bared head towards it and swore, in the sadness and silence of my desolate heart, that, to the full extent of the power which I believed was soon to be mine, I would take life for life and blood for blood, and I would give sorrow for sorrow and shame for shame, until I had paid to the full the debt which the long years of plunder and cruelty and oppression had heaped up against those who, from genera-tion to generation, had brought this shame and ruin on the once bright home of the Children of the Sun.

CHAPTER II

BROTHERS OF THE BLOOD

I SHALL not weary you who perchance may some day read this story of mine by dwelling on the sorrow and shame that filled me as I entered the foul, unlovely streets, and saw the filthy refuse in the squares of the city that I remembered so pure and bright and beautiful; nor yet by telling of the feelings that possessed me when I saw the poor remains of our desecrated temples, the places where our vanished palaces had stood, and the dismantled ruins of that mighty fortress of Sacsahuaman, which I had last seen standing palace-crowned and throned in all its grandeur high up above the city.

All this and more you who read must picture for yourselves, for I have greater things to tell of than the poor sorrows of a wanderer who had left his own age and his own kindred far behind him, and who had come back into a strange world to find his country a wilderness, and the children of his people the slaves of strangers.

It had been settled amongst us that, for the purpose for which we had come, it would be necessary to hire a house that should be at once commodious for our work, sufficiently removed from the city for privacy, and capable of defence against intruders if need be. The professor, being already known in Cuzco as a man of science and seeker after antiquities, and possessing, moreover, a special permit from the Government in Lima to travel and dwell in the interior, and make such searches as he thought fit, undertook the business of finding such a house. He made many journeys in quest of what he sought, and on these journeys Djama always accompanied him, since he had to see that the house chosen contained a chamber suitable for that precious work which he had undertaken to do in return for the share of treasure that I was to give to him.

And while these two were absent I at times wandered about the city with Joyful Star and Francis Hartness, who, it was plain to see, already looked with eyes of love and longing on her beauty, as in good truth I myself could have done had I dared, and could I have forgotten that older love of mine who still lay cold in her death-sleep in the cave by the lake yonder, over the mountains to the westward, whither I had already cast so many longing glances. But at other times I left them to go upon my own ways, for I had work on hand which, for the present, did not concern them.

I had by this time met and conversed with many of my people in their own language, which was that of the labouring classes of my own times, and from them I had learned that at a village called San Sebastian, through which we had passed, about two leagues to the south of the city, there still dwelt many families of Ayllos—that is to say, the descendants of those of the old noble Inca lineage, who had been permitted by their conquerors to settle here. So one morning I went to visit an old Indian—as they now called all our people—named Ullullo, with whom I had made acquaintance, and at his house I dressed myself in the native fashion—in an old shirt and short trousers, with sandals on my feet, and a broad-brimmed, fringed hat on my head, and covered myself with a faded poncho, and together we went on foot to San Sebastian, I looking no different from the rest of the Indians who were passing to and fro upon the road.

I had already seen, while riding through the village, that the people were different to those of all other villages that we had come through on the way. They were taller of stature, prouder of carriage, and fairer of face. The blood showed red in their cheeks through the light brown of their skin, and these signs had told me that if any remnant of the pure Inca race was left these must be they; and I was soon to have proof that it was so, although the children of those who had lived in palaces were now dwelling in huts of mud and reeds.

Ullullo led me first to the house of a man named Tupac Rayca, who was chief among the Indians of the town. He was great-grandson of that ill-fated Tupac-Amaru, who, as you know, had revolted many years before against the oppressors of his race, and for this, after being forced to watch the torture and murder of his wife in the square of Cuzco, had himself been torn limb from limb by horses.

We found him alone in a bare room in one of the better houses of the village. As he stood up to salute us it needed but a glance to tell me that in his veins at least the ancient blood of our race flowed well nigh as purely as it did in my own. Had it not been for the meanness of his clothing and the dull, brooding look on his noble features— the stamp of generations of oppression—I could have pictured him with the yellow Llautu * on

* The yellow Llautu, or fringed turban of wool, worn on the brows, was the distinguishing mark of the sacred Inca race. The scarlet was worn only by the reigning Inca—'Son of the Sun.' Its fringe, called the 'borla,' was mingled with threads of gold.

his brow, the golden image of the Sun on his girdled tunic, and the rainbow banner in his hand, standing amongst the guards of the great Huayna-Capac himself.

I asked Ullullo to leave us alone for a little while, and when he had gone I stepped forward, and, drawing myself up to my full height, I looked him in the eyes, and said in the tongue that was spoken only by those of the divine Inca race,—

'Tell me, Tupac-Rayca, does a remnant of the Children of the Sun still dwell in the Land of the Four Regions, and are they still faithful to the traditions of their race, and the faith of their ancestors?'

As the words left my lips he staggered back a pace or two with his hands clasped to his forehead, staring at me from under them as though—as in very truth I was—some spirit of the past stood re-embodied before him. Then, coming forward again and scanning me eagerly from head to foot, he whispered in the same tongue—by the Lord of Light how those familiar accents thrilled my ears as I heard them again after so long!

'Who are you—a stranger—that comes in the image of those long dead, to ask me such a question in the tongue that may only be spoken when none save those of the Blood are present?'

'One who is of the Blood himself!' I answered,

taking a stride towards him, and stretching out my hand. 'Fear not, Tupac-Rayca, son of him that suffered, I am a friend, and have come from afar to work as a friend with you and others of the Blood that may still be left in the land, with a great and holy purpose of which you shall know ere long.'

He grasped my hand and bowed over it in silence for a while. Then he stepped back and looked at me again, murmuring,—

'Can it be so? Has the divine Manco come back from the Mansions of the Sun to save the remnant of his children, or has Vilcaroya broken the bonds of his death-sleep and come to fulfil the oath he swore with Golden Star before the altar in the Sanctuary? I know all the Children of the Blood that are left in the land, and I have never seen your face before, yet you are of the Blood. Who are you—Lord?'

The last word seemed forced from his lips by some power other than his own will, and it sounded most pleasant to me, for it told me that, without knowing my name, and seeing me only as a stranger, he had recognised the stamp of my divine ancestry, and this promised well for the progress of the work I had in hand. I answered him kindly, and yet as one speaking to another who is scarce his equal, and said,—

My name matters not now or here, Tupac, for

we are but two, and I might lie to you, and you would have no proof of my truth or falsehood. But if you will do as I bid you, to-night you shall know and all shall be made plain and with ample proof. Are you willing to give me your aid?'

He picked up a rude hoe that stood in a corner of the room, and laying it across his shoulder after the manner of one who bears a burden, bowed his head and answered,—

'The Son of the Sun has but to speak, and I and all his slaves will obey.'

What he had done was an act of homage, which, in the olden time, was paid only to him who wore the imperial Llautu, and proved to me how faithfully the old traditions had been preserved in secret.

'That is well said, Tupac,' I replied, speaking now as a sovereign might speak to a faithful subject, 'and in the days to come fear not that I shall forget this, your first act of unasked-for homage. Now, hear me. Are there twenty men of the Blood in this village—men who are faithful and can be trusted even to the death?'

'There are five hundred here, Lord, and as many thousands within the valley, whose blood has flowed pure from the olden times, unpolluted by a single stain of Spanish dirt. What would you with them?'

'I asked not for hundreds or thousands,' I said, right glad at heart to hear such good tidings. 'For the present I need but a score, so do you choose me twenty of the noblest blood and the best judgment, and an hour before midnight let them be with you on the plain behind the Sacsahuaman. Let them come well provided with torches or candles, and tools, levers, and hammers and spades. Tell them what has passed between us, but nothing of the guesses that you may have made in your own mind while we have been talking, and leave the rest to me. Can you do that?'

'It shall be done, Lord,' he answered, still bending before me with the shaft of the hoe across his shoulders, 'and we will wait and toil in patience till the Son of the Sun shall please to reveal himself to the eyes of his servants.'

'Nor shall you have to wait long,' I said. 'Now put that off your back and take my hand again, for we are not Inca and servant yet, only two men of the Blood, and brothers of a fallen race who are joined together to perform a holy work. Now farewell, Tupac, till to-night. Choose your companions well, and fear not but that your services and your faithfulness shall have their due reward.'

He put his hand humbly and tremblingly into mine, bowing low over it, and so I left him, standing there with bent head, not daring to look up until the door closed behind me. Then Ullullo and I went back into the city, and as we crossed the great square on our way to Ullullo's house, I saw my four English friends standing among the market people by the fountain in the centre. We passed close to them, and I heard my name spoken by Joyful Star to her brother, who answered her and said,—

'I daresay we shall find he is making friends again with some of these filthy Indian compatriots of his.'

I hated him from that moment for his bitter words, and swore in my heart that some day he should pay for them, for I loved my people, and pitied them in their misery and degradation. I stopped beside them, and my heart was beating hard as I listened for what Joyful Star would say, and I have remembered her words, even as I have remembered his. She looked at him with the light of anger in her eyes and said,—

'For shame, Laurens! I couldn't have believed that you would have said such a thing. If you belonged to a race that had been enslaved and plundered by these brutes of Spaniards and Peruvians for three centuries and a half, do you think you would be any better than these poor fellows? And, besides, whatever they are, they are Vilcaroya's people, and he is our friend.'

I could have fallen on the stones and kissed

her feet for those sweet words of hers, and I moved away quickly for fear I should betray myself, and went with a swelling heart and mingled tears of love and anger in my eyes to old Ullullo's house, where I changed my clothes again, and then, as it was nearly dinner time, which, as you know, is in the evening in Spanish countries, I went back to the house where we were lodging, wondering what they would think if they could have understood the words that had passed between Tupac-Rayca and myself.

When I met them again I saw that they would willingly have learned what had become of me during the day, but I answered their inquiries by telling them nothing more and yet a great deal less than the truth, and saying that I had spent the day revisiting old scenes, and learning what I could of the present condition of my people. This satisfied them outwardly at least, though I saw a look in Djama's eyes which told me that he suspected more of the truth than it suited my purpose to tell him.

Then our conversation turned to the matter of procuring a house, such as I have spoken of, and the professor told me that he had heard of a hacienda, well built and solid, and standing in its own domain, about three leagues across the valley to the westward, on a secluded little plain among the hills, which would serve our purpose excellently;

but the owner of it wished to sell it, and 'with the stupidity of these Peruvians,' as he said, would not hire it out to us but would only sell it, and the price was twenty thousand soles, or dollars of Peru, which was two thousand pounds in English money.

'It is a great pity,' said the professor, when he had finished telling me about it, 'for it doesn't seem as though there was another house in the neighbourhood of Cuzco that would suit our purpose, and this one would do perfectly.'

'Of course, if the fellow won't let it there's no use thinking any more about the matter, for two thousand pounds is entirely out of the question. It seems to me that the expedition will be quite expensive enough without the luxury of buying houses at fancy prices.'

It was Djama who spoke. No one else at our table could have spoken like that. I heard him in silence, for I could not trust myself to speak for the anger that was rising within me. I saw Joyful Star raise her eyelids and look at him with a swift glance that meant much; but she, too, said nothing; and then, looking at me, he spoke again and said,—

'Of course, if His Highness'—for so he always spoke of me when no strangers were present—'would just unlock one of those treasure-houses of his, the matter would be easy enough, but I suppose that's outside the contract.'

I still kept silence, knowing as I did what the night was to bring forth. But Francis Hartness answered for me, and said,—

'I don't think you can quite put it that way, Djama, if you'll excuse me saying so. If I am not mistaken, it has been clearly understood that the first treasure-house to be unlocked is the one that holds Vilcaroya's greatest treasure—his wife—and what you say seems to suggest—'

'It is enough!' I said, unconsciously speaking in my growing anger in the same imperious tone that I had used but a few hours before to Tupac. 'Let the house be bought. I will charge myself with the cost, and I will be the debtor of my friends no longer.'

They stared at me as I spoke, for hitherto I had spoken to them as a child rather than as a man ; as an inferior, rather than as an equal. I saw a smile that was not pleasant to look upon pass swiftly over Djama's mouth, but he kept silence, and the professor said to me,—

'Are you really in earnest, Vilcaroya? You know, according to our bargain, we have no claim on you until our part of the work is done. None of us have any desire to learn your secrets.'

'I am not talking of secrets,' I said, breaking into his speech, 'and one of my race does not speak to make a liar of himself. What I say I can do and will, for I wish the work to begin at once. Do you think I have not waited long enough for my beloved, my sister and my wife ? '

' Your what l ' cried Joyful Star, rising suddenly from her seat, and staring at me with fixed and wide-opened eyes. ' Your sister! Oh, Vilcaroya, surely this is not true!' and as she said this I saw her cheeks grow pale and her lips tremble.

' Yes,' I answered, ' it is true. Why should I lie to my new sister and friend, Joyful Star ? Golden Star was the daughter of my father, the great Huayna-Capac, though our mothers were not the same.'

I had no time to finish my speech, for with a look of unutterable horror in her eyes, which pierced me to the heart and seemed to sever it in twain, she cried,—

' Oh, no, no ! that is too horrible ! I don't want to hear any more. I will go back to England to-morrow. Laurens, come to my room ; I want to speak to you at once.'

So saying, she went to the door and opened it and went out, followed by her brother, who looked at me as he passed me with a look which I never forgot or forgave, for it was like the words that I had heard him say to her in the square.

' What is this ? ' I said to the professor when the door had closed behind them. ' What have

I said or done that Joyful Star should look with horror upon me and say such cruel words?'

I saw him exchange glances full of meaning with the English soldier before he answered me; and then, leaning his arms on the table in front of him, he said, in that quiet, calm voice of his,—

'My dear Vilcaroya, it is a very strange thing, and, as far as Miss Djama is concerned, perhaps, a very great pity that this has never come out before, for without knowing it you have given her a shock that may have very painful consequences. No, don't interrupt me now, for the sooner I can make you understand the meaning of your words to her the better. It is this way: we know, of course, that in your day and among your people sister-marriage was held to be the most sacred of all marriages. We know that from such a marriage only might spring the wearer of the imperial Borla, but to us the idea is so unutterably horrible and revolting that of all the crimes that could be committed by one of our race that would be the most fearful. It cannot even be discussed amongst us, and yet you, in the most perfect innocence, have spoken of it in the presence— Good Heavens, Hartness! what is to be done? Do you think Miss Djama was really in earnest when she talked of going back to England to-morrow? It is impossible— it would ruin everything!'

I kept silence, for my sorrow and wonder were too great for words, but I listened eagerly for what Francis Hartness would say in reply.

'She was in earnest when she spoke,' he said, as quietly as the professor had spoken; 'but, if the doctor has as much sense as I give him credit for, she will have seen the thing in a different light by this time. Of course, she has read Prescott, and she really knows as much about the marriage customs of the ancient Incas as we do. In fact, to tell you the truth'—and as he said this I saw him frown, and an angry light came into his eyes that I had never seen in them before—'I really can hardly understand how, knowing that as she does know it, she can have been as horrified as she certainly was. She knows perfectly well that Vilcaroya has come at a single step, as it were, from his age into ours, and so must have brought all the ideas and beliefs of his time and his people with him. Depend upon it, a little reflection will very soon show her that, horrible and all as the idea must naturally have appeared to her at the first shock of hearing it, from Vilcaroya's point of view there is nothing in it but what is perfectly natural and proper. Now, to my mind, the matter is much more sad and serious for Vilcaroya himself than for anyone else.'

As he said this he turned from the professor to me and went on, addressing me in a tone so frank and kindly that ever afterwards I looked upon him as my friend and my brother,—

'It's not a pleasant thing for me to say, and it must, of course, be a very painful one for you to hear; still, it has got to be said some time or other, and, unless I am wrong in what I think of you, I believe you are man enough to hear it and to agree with me that it had better be said now than later on, when the saying of it might be tenfold more painful both to you and us.'

'Say on,' I said shortly. 'Your tongue is straight and your eyes look into mine as those of a friend should look. I am listening.'

'I would wish for no better friend than you, Vilcaroya, after that, for I know what you mean. Now, what I have to say is this. We know, of course, that you look upon yourself as doubly married to this love of yours, who is dead and, like you, may yet be alive again. You are bound to her, not only by a marriage which, in the time that it took place, was perfectly lawful and natural, but also by the oath that you took together. But you have come back to the world in another age and among another people, and now that form of marriage is looked upon by all civilised humanity, not only as unlawful, but, as the professor has just said, unnatural and horrible beyond conception.

'Therefore, if Golden Star is restored to life, for you to love her, save as a brother, or for you to consummate the union which, as you have told us, began and ended before the altar of the Sun, would be to make not only yourself, but your— your sister, Golden Star, as well, looked upon with horror and loathing by every civilised man and woman who knew your story. I am speaking strongly, because it is necessary.

'You might succeed in all your aims, you might realise every ambition of your life, and yet I tell you it is Heaven's own truth, that if you took Golden Star to sit beside you on the throne of the Incas as your wife and queen, you would place her upon a pinnacle of infamy which men would spit upon and women turn their backs on. The reward of all your labours, the price of all your treasures, no matter how great they might be, would be nothing but a curse that would fall heavily on you, but a thousand times more heavily on the woman whom you have loved best in all the world.'

He stopped, and they both sat and looked at me in silence, awaiting for me to answer him. As for me, I felt my spirit wandering over a bare wilderness where all was dark.

I knew that he had spoken truth, strange as the truth seemed to me, for no man could have heard his voice and seen the steady light in his eyes, without knowing that he was a true man, and so spoke the truth. The moments passed, and I could still find no words to say. Then the silence was broken by the opening of the door, and Djama came in and said,—

'My sister wishes you to excuse her coming back to the table. Of course, I have explained matters to her, and I think she now sees them in a different light, but for some reason or other she seems strangely shaken. You know how extremely sensitive she is, and so, as her doctor, as well as her brother, I have sent her to bed. She wasn't really fit to come back after what has happened, and a night's rest will be the best thing in the world for her. I suppose you two have explained things to His Highness as well, eh?'

'Yes,' I said, rising from my seat. 'It has been explained to me. I do not understand all now, but I must think, and think alone, so I will go.'

Then I went to Francis Hartness and held out my hand to him and said, after the fashion of the English,—

'Good-night, Captain Hartness. You have wounded me sorely with your words, yet you have spoken them as only a friend could speak them. From now till the day of my death or yours, Vilcaroya Inca is your friend, and all his people are your servants.'

Then I took my hand from his, and bowing
farewell to the others, walked swiftly out of the
room and got my cloak, and went out into the
city to think in silence by myself over the strange
and terrible things that I had heard, and to calm
my spirit before I went to do the work which, in
a few hours, would be awaiting me on the hills
behind the Sacsahuaman.

CHAPTER III

IN THE HALL OF GOLD

I WENT first to Ullullo's house and changed my clothing, so that I might the more easily lose myself among the hundreds of Indians about the streets of the city, for something told me that Djama might make an attempt to discover the meaning of what I had said about the house by following me and learning, if possible, the secret of my movements; for he must have known that, being without money as I was, save for the few dollars that the professor had lent me, it would not be possible for me to do as I had said, unless one, at least, of the hiding-places of the old treasures was within easy reach so that I could take sufficient gold out of it by the next day to fulfil my promise.

When I changed my clothes I put a dagger into my belt, and a revolver, which Francis Hartness had already taught me how to use, into a case slung at my hip, and hidden by my jacket and the long folds of my poncho. Then I went back into the great square, and across it up the street in which we had our lodgings. As I passed the house I saw Djama standing in the archway leading into the courtyard, smoking a cigar. I turned and looked him in the face as I went by, slouching and trailing my sandalled feet after the fashion of the natives. He looked at me, but I saw no recognition in his eyes. Then as I walked on there came a thought to me.

I hurried to Ullullo's house once more and brought him back with me, telling him on the way what I wanted him to do for me. When we reached the house again we saw Djama standing in the courtyard, and Ullullo, doing as I had bid him, went in to him, and told him in Spanish, which I could not speak, that if he would give him ten dollars he should learn the secret of my goings and comings, and where I was to find the gold with which to pay for the hacienda. Djama instantly promised him the money, as I thought he would, and Ullullo told him to be at the end of the street which is now called El Triunfo at eleven o'clock that night. He was to come alone, for if anyone came with him he would learn nothing. As you will soon see, I had two objects to serve in doing this.

When Ullullo came back and told me that

Djama would be there, I bade him wait for me at the same place and hour, and then I went away alone out of the city and up a path which led towards the mountains to the north. There, alone and in silence, I communed with my own soul, at first in sorrow, yet slowly becoming more and more peaceful in heart, even as one who is told that he is to die on a certain day first rages against his doom and then learns to contemplate with calmness that which there is no hope of escaping. The words of the professor and Francis Hartness had shown me that in the world to which I had returned my sister Golden Star could now never be my wife and queen, and the more I pondered on what they had said, the more plainly it appeared to me that this was the truth, however bitter it might seem.

Yet there was something else in my heart, although at that time I did not dare even to let my inmost thoughts dwell upon it, which in some way dulled the pain of the blow that had fallen upon me, and reconciled me to the parting which in one sense must now be eternal. The longer I pondered the more deeply did that look of horror which I had seen in the eyes of Joyful Star burn into my soul, and the more clearly did the words that she had spoken ring in my ears. She had said that it was horrible and that it was impossible, and she was to me as one of those bright angels who, according to our ancient faith, awaited the heroes and sages of our race in the Mansions of the Sun—a being so far above me that I could look upon her only as a mortal might look from afar upon a daughter of the Celestials.

Thus, musing in silence and solitude on the wild mountain-side, now looking back into my distant past, and now hazarding a glance into the fast-approaching future, the hours slipped by quickly for me, and I heard the bells of the churches — bells which they had told me had been cast out of the copper and gold and silver that our conquerors had taken from our temples and palaces—chiming the half-hour before eleven.

So I turned back to the city, and made haste to the place where Djama and Ullullo would be waiting for me. I found them there talking together, and without discovering myself to Djama, I told Ullullo in Quichua to follow me with the Englishman. Then I went on swiftly along the rivulet of Tullamayo, past the terrace of Rocca Inca, and along the smooth, dark wall of what had once been the Yachahuasi, or College of the Youths, and so out of the city and the gorge of the little river Rodadero. Then, with the two still following me a few yards behind, I climbed the lower terraces of the Colcompata, or the Granaries, where the divine Manco built his first palace, and then on up the hillside to the Tiupunco, or Gate of Sand, which led through the fragments of what had once been the outer wall of the great fortress, and so on to the little level pampa of the Rodadero, which was my meeting - place with Tupac.

Now as I went I began to sing one of our ancient songs, which was the signal that I had agreed upon with Tupac, and presently, one after another, silent, stealthy forms crept out from the angles of the great zig-zag wall and came towards me. One of them, taller than the rest, threw an iron bar that he was carrying across his shoulders, and came and stood before me with bowed-down head, waiting for me to speak. I knew that it was Tupac, and I said to him,—

'Are the Children of the Sun ready to do the bidding of his Son?'

'They are, Lord!' he replied. 'Here are twenty who have sworn by the heart of the divine Manco to do all things lawful and unlawful, even to the death, at the bidding of him who shall prove himself to be the true heir of the royal Llautu.'

'It is good,' I said, 'and the proof shall soon be given. Now, take the stranger yonder; do him no harm, but bind his eyes so that he cannot see, and tie his hands behind him. Then follow me.'

Instantly the stealthy forms closed around

Djama. Not a word was spoken save his startled, angry exclamation, which was soon stifled, and then they brought him along after me, I going first and Tupac following close behind me. Like a string of shadows we moved across the plain past the great carved rock which is still called the Inca's Seat, and over the ridge of the Sliding Stones and down into the valley beyond, which is thickly strewn with great rock-masses carved into seats, and altars, and baths, and chambers, of which no man knows the origin, and which were ancient when Manco-Capac and Mama-Occlu first came into the land.

The greatest of these is a high white rock carved all over into steps and seats and altars and basins, which are said to have been made to catch the blood of the living sacrifices that were offered up here by a race of men whose name has been forgotten. It is called in our language the Sayacusca, or Tired Stone, for an old tradition says that ages ago it was brought from the mountains by the toil of ten thousand men, and when it reached its present place it rolled over and killed three hundred of them, and could never be moved again upon its journey.

On the south side of this there is a great cleft from the top to the bottom, and up the sides of this cleft are the two halves of a stairway, which was carved there before some earthquake rent the stone in twain, and under this is a deep dark pool of water. At the entrance to the cleft I stopped and beckoned to the others to come round me. Then I told them that they were about to see that which no man then alive on earth had ever seen, and made all swear by the Glory of the Sun that each and every one of them would slay without pity him who revealed anything seen or heard that night, even though he were his own brother, or his own father, or his own son. As for Djama, they held him there bound and blindfolded amongst them, and when he tried to speak they stopped his mouth at my bidding, for I had told them that I would be answerable for him, since I had brought him here for my own purposes.

Then I made two of the men stretch a cord tightly across the mouth of the cleft close down to the ground, and to the middle of this I tied another cord, and stretched it out straight twelve foot-lengths from the centre, and here I bade them clear away the bushes, and dig. Then axe and hoe and spade went to work. In that clear air, and under that cloudless sky, the stars gave light enough to work by, and soon a space had been cleared, and a round hole about three feet across was being dug down through the loose, rocky soil.

When it was about half the depth of a man the spades struck on the solid rock below, and could go no farther. When Tupac told me of this, I, who had been standing by the cleft, looking—full of strange thoughts—down into the dark pool of water, called the man who had been digging out of the hole, and, taking an iron bar from Tupac, I dropped into it.

I sought about the bottom with my hands for a few moments till I found the outline of a squared stone that had been let into the rock. In the centre of this I found a hole, out of which I picked the dirt with my dagger. Then, putting the end of my iron bar into it, I pulled, and the stone turned over on a hinge, leaving an opening half its size. Down this I thrust my arm, and found a chain of copper which hung down into a deep well below. I pulled this with all my strength until something gave way at the bottom, then I drew the chain up, and cast my iron bar under it across the hole. As I did this, I heard the deep, smothered roar of waters rushing away far below me into the bowels of the earth.

Then I got out of the hole and went back to the cleft. I lit a candle and looked down at the pool. It was no longer stagnant now, but seething and eddying like a whirlpool. I beckoned to Tupac, who was standing a little way behind me, and as he came and looked over my shoulder I pointed down into the dark gulf, out of which the bottom was rapidly falling, and said,—

'See, the waters are opening the way by which the Son of the Sun shall go into his kingdom. Watch now, and listen!'

'Son of the Sun and Lord of the Four Regions, it is true!' he whispered as the waters eddied round faster and faster, and gurgled and rattled down into some unknown abyss. Soon they vanished altogether, leaving only a dark, black, and seemingly fathomless cavern in the place where they had been. I waited until the sound of the last gurgle had died away in the depths, and then I turned to Tupac and said,—

'The way is open. Tell Ullullo to bring the lantern and light it. There must be no other light. You and the rest follow me, and let two strong men bring the stranger.'

He did as I bade him, and when I had lit the lantern I cast its rays about the gulf beneath me till I found the continuation of the broken stairway above, and then picking my way carefully down the dank, slimy steps, I led the way into the heart of the rock, the rest following, guided by the spreading ray of light in front of me.'

I counted fifty steps, and then stopped and turned sharply to the right. The fiftieth step ended against a wall of rock, still dripping with the water that was running down from the arched roof of the chamber. I measured ten spans with my hand from the wall where the steps ended, and made a mark with my dagger on the rock. Then from the floor I measured eight spans in a line across the mark. Where the eighth span ended I made another mark, and with the help of my lantern I found a silver socket let into the rock. It was a plate with a hole in the centre large enough to admit the iron bar which I had brought for the purpose. I put it in, and whispering to Tupac to help me, we gripped the bar, and after two or three hard pulls felt it coming towards us.

A great slab of rock, which fitted into the wall with all the perfection that our old Inca masons could give it, turned on a central hinge, leaving a space that two men could have walked through abreast,

'Go in,' I said to Tupac, 'and let all follow you.'

He obeyed, and standing by the opening with a ray of my lantern shooting across it, I watched them file past one by one until all had gone in. Then I followed, and as I crossed the threshold set my shoulder against the edge of the slab and pushed it back into its place.

Now I covered my lantern with my poncho and cried aloud in the darkness,—

'Let the torches be got ready, but let no light be struck till that which is to be revealed may be seen.'

A low murmur answered me, and then, still keeping my lantern hidden, I felt my way along the wall, treading softly as a mountain lion approaching its prey, until I had counted forty paces. The fortieth brought me to a doorway, through which I turned. Five paces more brought me to another turning, ten more to the end of the passage, and then I uncovered my light and found myself in a little square chamber hewn out of the rock and surrounded with stone chests covered with lids of copper.

In the centre of the chamber stood a smaller one, all of metal. I set my lantern down on one of the others so that the light fell across this one; then I raised the lid, and there before me lay, perfect as they had been on the day when Anda-Huillac, last High Priest of the Sun, had laid them there, the imperial robes and insignia that had last been worn by the ill-fated Huascar, son of the great Huayna-Capac.

Quickly throwing off the mean garments that I wore, I dressed myself in them. Then, binding the golden sandals on my feet, and clasping the long mantle emblazoned in gold and jewels with the symbols of the Sun and his sister-wife the Moon across my shoulders, I wound the scarlet Llautu around my head, with the crimson fringe of the Borla interlaced with gold falling upon my brow, and then, closing the chest, I took up my lantern and went back along the passages I had traversed.

In the middle of the last one I put my lantern down with the glass against the wall, and feeling my way into the doorway, which opened on to the chamber in which the others were awaiting me, I cried, in a voice that echoed strangely through the great chamber,—

'Let the torches be kindled, and let the Children of the Sun look upon their Lord !'

I heard a shuffling of feet and a whispering of many voices. Then lights were struck, and I stepped back quickly into the shadow of the doorway. I saw the glow of light grow into a glare that was flashed back in a thousand many-coloured rays from the walls of the chamber. I heard a deep, low cry of wonder, and then I strode out into the midst and said,—

'I am he who went into the shadows at the bidding of our Father the Sun, and by his will I have returned to bring deliverance to his children !'

For one moment of affrighted amazement they stared wide-eyed at me standing there before them, as though Huayna-Capac himself had returned from the Mansions of the Sun to resume his sceptre and his crown. Then, with one accord, they sank on their knees before me, holding their torches above their bent heads and murmuring,—

' Hail, Son of the Sun and deliverer of his children, who hast come to bring the daylight back to the long-darkened Land of the Four Regions ! '

I looked at them and saw Djama standing erect, still bound and blindfold, in the midst of them. I went through the kneeling forms to him, and taking the bandage from his eyes stepped back, and while he was blinking at the light of the torches, said to him in English,—

' Look about you, Laurens Djama, and tell me if you believe now that I, the friend of the filthy Indians whom you despise, can do that which I have said ? '

He was still half dazzled by the glare of the torches and the thousand rays of many colours that were flashing about him. Wherever his wondering glance fell it saw great golden plates covering the walls, thick-set with jewels, and in front of him, piled up against the end wall of the chamber, a shining heap of gold bars in the shape of a pyramid reaching to the roof of the chamber, and on either side of this, half way up, was a great image of the Sun, like to that which in the olden times stood above the altar in the sanctuary of the great temple of Cuzco, each with its centre fashioned as a human face, with great flashing diamonds for eyes, with lips of rubies, and long pendants of emeralds hanging from the ears, and all round a hundred curving rays of gold edged and lined with jewels.

He stared about him, open-eyed and open-mouthed with amazement. Then his eyes fell on me, and he started forward and stared me in the face for a moment. Then he gasped,—

'Vilcaroya, is it you, or am I dreaming? Where have you brought me to?'

'To one of the treasure-houses that you so longed to see,' I said, 'so that you might see and believe that I told you no idle tale, and that I can perform my promise if you can perform yours.'

Then I turned my back on him and went to the foot of the pyramid, and, taking my place in front of it, I said to those who still knelt before me in silence,—

'Let those of his children who are faithful to their Father the Sun rise and come without falsehood in their hearts, and say if they now believe that that which was foretold long ago, when the darkness fell over the land, has in very truth come to pass.'

They rose from their knees and came towards me in a half circle, carrying their torches. They stopped about five paces from me, looking at me through a little space with wondering eyes full of worship. Then they bowed their heads again, and Tupac came from the midst of them, and, casting himself prone at my feet, yet not daring even to touch my sandals, said in a broken voice,—

'Son of the Sun, heir of heaven and lord of earth, we have seen thy wisdom and thy majesty. None but one of thy royal line—nay, none but thee, oh, Vilcaroya, son of Huayna-Capac, and brother of Huascar, last of the Incas, could have known the secret that thou hast brought with thee from the past into the present. We are thy children and thy slaves, and all the men of the Blood that are left in the Land of the Four Regions shall hail thee lord as we do, and own no other master save thee, Vilcaroya Inca, from now until the hour when their father, the Lord of Life, shall call them back to the Mansions of the Sun. We are thine, and we will serve thee, ourselves and our wives and our children, as our fathers served thy father in the days when there was yet peace and happiness in the land.'

'And if ye are but faithful,' I said, 'and if the Lord, my father, who rules the day, and his sister, my mother, who rules the night, shall give me strength and wisdom to use the power that is mine, I will give you back peace and happiness, and the stranger and the oppressor shall be driven from the land, and the homes of the Children of the Sun shall again be full of light. Rise now, Tupac, and let ten of the men give their torches to the others and make ready to do my bidding.'

He rose, and it was done.   Then I called Djama to me and said,—

'What you have seen here to-night is a dream. When your eyes open again on the outer world, remember what I have said. Your hand has brought me from the grave to the throne, and you must obey me as these do.   Let me but know that you have spoken one word, even to Joyful Star herself, concerning what you have seen here to-night, and I will show you how an Inca deals with one who dares to disobey him. Keep silence and have patience, and perform that which you have promised, and you shall go back to your own land loaded with gold and jewels.   Fail, and the fragments of your body shall be sent north and south and east and west throughout the Land of the Four Regions, and your name shall be one of shame in the ears of my people for ever.'

For a moment he looked me in the eyes, and I saw his lips moving as though he was striving to shape some answer to my words.   Then his face grew grey, and his knees shook as he stood. Then I called to Tupac, and bade him bind his eyes again and lead him away, and as soon as his sight was taken from him I bade the ten men who had given up their torches take off their ponchos and fill them with as many of the golden bars as each one could carry, and when

F

this was done, I ordered all the torches save one
to be extinguished. This one I took, and went
with it into the passage where I had left my
lantern. Then I dashed it against the wall and
vanished into the darkness.

I took my lantern, and hiding the light carefully, went back to the little chamber, where I
took off my robes and sandals and the imperial
Llautu, and put them back into the chest. Then
I put on my mean attire again and went back into
the Hall of Gold. Signing to the others to follow
me, I turned the stone door on its pivot again,
and watched them file past me as before. Then,
going out last, I closed the portal after me and
lighted them up the steps with my lantern.

When we all once more stood in the open air by
the cleft I went to the hole and released the chain.
Instantly the roar of waters broke out again, and
I bade them fill the hole up and put turf over it,
and trample it down and scatter the bushes over
it ; and that being done, we took our way back
again across the plain towards the fortress, still
leading Djama blindfold in our midst.

We took him by the gate of Viracocha into the
fortress, across its upper part, where the three
crosses stood, and down on to the zigzag road
which leads into the eastern part of the city, and
there we unbound his eyes, and I bade him go to
the house and make ready to receive me early in

the morning, telling our friends that I should arrive with some packages of Indian merchandise and metals from one of my mines, for, as I should have told you before, I had come to Cuzco in the character of an owner of mines who had lived long in Europe and had returned to supervise the working of my property.

I and Tupac and his companions then went back into the hills, and without entering the city made our way by twos and threes into the village of San Sebastian. We met at Tupac's house, and there I explained to them as much of my plans and purposes as I thought fit for them to know, and showed them that the time was not yet come for them to make use of the treasures that I would share with them. But to each man I gave two pounds' weight of gold to be left in Tupac's care till it could be taken into the cities of the south and there changed for silver coins. Then I had a list made of their names, and promised them, after reminding them of their oaths, that when I once more sat on the throne of the divine Manco, their fidelity should be well remembered.

The next morning we loaded the gold in bales of the coca-leaf, great quantities of which are taken every day into Cuzco, upon four mules, and these I sent to our house while I went back with Ullullo and put on my English clothing. Then I followed, and found that the bags of coca had already arrived. They were carried up to my own room, and there, in the presence of Djama and Joyful Star, the professor and Francis Hartness, I took out the gold ingots and built them up in a pyramid before them.

I could see from their amazement that, whether from fear or faith, Djama had obeyed me, and said nothing of what he had seen during the night. As for me, I said but little. I gave them the gold, and that day the professor and Djama, acting as my agents, sold it to some of the merchants of Cuzco as the product of my mines. The price was more than twice as much as was needed for the hacienda, so with the rest I discharged my debt and made myself once more a free man.

There is no need for me to dwell upon our dealings with the owner of the hacienda, and therefore it will suffice for me to say, before ten days more had passed the purchase-money had been paid, we had taken up our abode there, and installed Joyful Star as housewife, with faithful servants chosen by myself from among the Children of the Blood. Djama, who had been strangely silent and reserved with all of us since the lesson I had taught him in the Hall of Gold, had taken possession of the chamber which was devoted to his uses, and had put all his apparatus in order for the great work that was to be done there.

So on the fourteenth day, such was the power of my gold and of my longings, all things were ready, and at daybreak on the fifteenth day we rode at the head of our little mule train out of the courtyard of the hacienda on our way to the resting-place of Golden Star.

CHAPTER IV

THE SISTER STARS

FOR five long days we travelled slowly and toilfully on our way from the valley of Cuzco to that other where Golden Star lay sleeping beside the lake. Over high plains and pleasant valleys, through deep, dark gorges and ravines, to whose lowest depths the sun but seldom reaches, and then but for an hour or two, along narrow pathways cut into the living rock on the mountain side, with precipices on one hand falling thousands of feet into the dark abysses, where the torrents roared and foamed, and on the other the great rock-walls of the mountain soaring up into the sky yet more thousands of feet above us.

I saw the mighty crests of Saljantai and Umantai rising snow-crowned from earth to heaven, unchanged in their eternal grandeur since the long-distant day on which I had last beheld them. I rode with saddened heart past the ruins of Lima Tambo, remembering how fair and stately a city it had been in the days before the plunderer and the oppressor came. We toiled slowly over the great, sharp-ridged range which parts the waters of the Vilcamayo from those of the Apurimac—the 'Great Speaker'—then, descending again by the gorge of the river which is now called the Rio de la Banca, we came to the long bridge which swings in mid-air from rock to rock across the chasm through which the Great Speaker rolls his swift, roaring flood.

Its cables were loosened and its floorway broken, for, like all things else in the land, the Spaniards had suffered it to fall well nigh to ruin ; and, as I led Joyful Star across it by the hand, I thought of what it had been in the olden times, when not a rope or a stick was suffered to be out of place, and when the Son of the Sun had been borne across it in his golden travelling litter, with long processions of his adoring people going before and behind him, strewing his way with flowers, and waking the echoes of these gloomy gorges with the melody of their songs and laughter.

From here we journeyed on, ever facing the setting sun, for two days more, still winding higher and higher up into the mountains, until at length, on the third evening, I, riding alone many yards in front of the others, found the sign that I was looking for—a rock with three seats carved on the top of it—and turned my mule from the track and rode over the rough, stony ground up the side of the mountain until what looked from the road a single rock-built peak opened into two. I beckoned to the others to follow me, and when they came up I said to the professor,—

' Do you know where you are now? Have you ever been here before ? '

He looked about him and shook his head, saying,—

' This may have been the place where we got off the road when my mule gave out, but I don't recognise it. Do you mean that we are near the valley ? '

' Yes,' I said. ' Do you not remember seeing yonder two peaks from the shore of the lake near where you found me ? '

He looked at them for a moment, and then said,—

' Yes, I remember them ; but they don't look the same, and I don't believe I could find my way back into the valley from here to save my life. It's very strange how I can have forgotten it so completely.'

I smiled as he said this, knowing that I had brought them purposely many miles out of the way by which he had found the valley by accident, for I had no desire that the way should be known to any but myself and those I had chosen from among the remnant of the Children of the Blood. Then I bade them follow me again, and once more rode on alone ahead, for, as you may well believe, I was too full of my own thoughts and hopes and fears to be in any mood for conversation, even with Joyful Star herself. They, too, talked but little, and as we rode on in the deepening gloom amid the solemn silence and the gaunt grandeur of the mountains, their words became fewer and fewer, till at length thought took the place of speech, and the silence was broken by no sound save the patter of the mules' feet and the rattle of stones under their iron-shod hoofs.

Hour after hour I led them on, turning from valley to valley on the road that was visible only to my own eyes, and ever rising higher and higher towards the twin peaks that now stood out dark and sharp against the starry sky. At last, when our watches were nearly marking ten o'clock, I stopped before a cliff covered with bushes and creeping grasses, and calling Tupac to me, I bade him seek for an opening under these.

He groped about among the bushes for a while, and then suddenly, with a short cry of surprise, he vanished, as it seemed, through the face of the rock itself. I dismounted and followed him, and found him standing behind the bushes, facing a square doorway cut in the rock and lined with masonry. Behind it, and closing it completely, was a great slab of dressed stone. Down the sides of the doorway were two square pillars of stone, and in the middle of one, to the left hand, three little lines had been cut about a finger's breadth apart, but so faintly that only one who knew they were there could find them.

I stretched a string across from the middle one of these to the right-hand pillar, and where the string ended in the centre of the pillar I felt with my finger-tips and found a little circle about as big round as an English two-shilling piece. Tupac had in his hand the iron rod that I had used on the Rodadero. I took it from him, and, pressing the end against the circle, told him to push with me, and, to his wonder, the rod sank, seemingly, into the solid stone, forcing out a bolt which had been fitted so cunningly into the pillar that the end of it looked no more than a circle traced on the face of it.

When we had pushed the rod in about six inches I bade Tupac help me to pull it round towards the door. The pillar turned on a central hinge as we did so, and the great stone slab swung back by its own weight, which we had thus released, opening the entrance to a tunnel high enough for a man to walk through erect. This tunnel sloped somewhat sharply upwards, and looking up it I could see, shining in the clear sky beyond the upper entrance, the stars that I knew were reflected in the still waters of the little lake by which Golden Star was sleeping the sleep out of which we had come to wake her.

As the passage was not large enough for the mules to go through with their burdens, I bade my men unload them and carry their loads through into the valley. Then we followed, leading our own animals by the bridle, and after us the cargo-mules were driven through. The load of one of them was a long, narrow case of wood like that in which the professor had taken my own dead body to London, but this was thickly and softly padded inside with wool, and lined with white linen, and at one end was a little pillow of the softest down, on which the head of Golden Star would soon be resting.

As soon as we were all standing outside the upper mouth of the tunnel I looked at Joyful Star and said,—

' Is not this a fitting resting-place even for the daughter of kings? Are not the stars bright in the heavens and on the bosom of the lake? Are not the mountains great, and strong, and silent? Do they not guard her couch well, and does not the snowy peak of Umantai yonder point the straight way to the Mansions of the Sun, where the soul of Golden Star is even now waiting for the arts of your brother to call it back to earth as he called mine?'

'Yes,' she said, looking about her, first at the stars and then at the vast shapes of the mountains which loomed huge and dim on every side. 'Yes, Vilcaroya, it is a good place for sleep, but—is not the world beyond a good place to wake in? Have *you* not found it so?'

I caught the gleam of her eyes in the starlight as she looked towards me saying this, and, by the glory of the Sun, had we stood alone where we were, I might have forgotten all save the knowledge that I was the lawful lord of all this land, and that she was there in the midst of it with me. For the instant I had gone back to my old life, with all its old-world thoughts and customs, and then, before I could answer her, my dreaming soul was called back to the present by the cold, quiet voice of her brother saying,—

'I don't think that very many would find the world an unpleasant place to wake in, either for the first or second time, if they could also wake up lord of illimitable treasures as Vilcaroya here has done. But come, Your Highness, and you, professor, it is getting late. Don't you think it is time to be thinking about camping?'

The matter-of-fact words scattered my dreams in an instant, and I woke from them into the present. I bade Tupac have the animals tethered and fed, and the tents we had brought with us pitched in the most sheltered place he could find ; and while they were doing this, and Djama and the others were busy seeing that the work was done to their satisfaction, I went to Ruth and said— my words, which I strove so hard to keep steady, trembling with I know not how many mingled passions,—

'Will Joyful Star come with me and see the place where her sister and mine is lying, waiting to come forth and greet her ?'

'Your sister, Vilcaroya?' she said, turning her face up to me so that the starlight shone upon its fairness and lost itself in the lustrous depths of her eyes. 'Do you mean your sister only—not—your—'

'No,' I said, 'not my wife, for I have thought upon your words and pondered them deeply; and though they wounded me sorely at first, yet now I see that they were wise and just, like all the other words that Joyful Star has spoken to me. I have learned that lesson, like many others which you have taught me. That bridal of ours is already to me a dream of the long-lost past, the vision of a time that is dead and a people that is no more. When Golden Star wakes, if she ever does, I will greet her as a sister and a friend, as one of my own people who has come back to me out of my own times, and she shall help me in the work that I swore with her to do—but that is all ; and I will find others of the Blood who shall sit upon the restored throne of my ancestors, and be the parents of the generations of Incas that shall come after me.'

' What do you mean, Vilcaroya ? ' she said, in a voice that was half angry and half fearful. ' Do you mean—no, I cannot say it—for I am sure you do not mean that.'

' How could that be ? ' I answered, guessing her meaning. ' Is it not *you* who have taught me the ways and thoughts of the world into which I have come back? No, what I mean is that I am not the only one now alive in whose veins the old blood of the Incas flows. Tupac, yonder, is the son of the son of the son of that Tupac-Amaru who died torn asunder in the square of Cuzco, because he had dared to raise the Rainbow Banner in the Land of the Four Regions, and called the Children of the Sun to revolt against their oppressors. He, more blessed than I who am his lord, has both wife and child, and if the prophecy is to be fulfiled, and I am to reign in the City of the Sun, then I will take his firstborn and instruct him in all the lore of our people and the duties of their ruler, and if he proves worthy he shall wear the Llautu after me.'

She looked up at me again as I ceased speaking, just one swift, bright glance that seemed to pierce to the most secret depths of my soul, and read the unuttered thoughts that were hidden there, thoughts which I did not dare to speak even to myself in the loneliest hour of my musings. Then she looked down again, and side by side we walked in silence round the shore of the lake until I stopped in front of a great black cliff that jutted out from the mountain side and hung impending over the dark, still waters of the lake. I pointed into the black shadows in which its base was hidden, and said,—

'There lies Golden Star, and there I lay beside her through all the long years that were to pass from the night when I pledged my troth with her before the Altar of the Sun until this night when I stand with you, Joyful Star, a new being in a new world, before her resting-place.'

'Is it really true?' she said, stopping as she spoke, and staring straight before her into the darkness. 'Is it really true that you, who are standing alive and strong here beside me, lay there under that great rock for all those years, while ten generations of men and women were born, and lived and died, and the whole world changed again and again? And is the Golden

Star lying in there now really the Golden Star you have told me so much of, and I have thought about until she seems to me more like some living friend that I have known and loved, than a dead body that has been in the grave for more than three hundred years? Is it really true, Vilcaroya, or have we all only been dreaming some wild dream, like that Frankenstein story that I was telling you the other day?'

As she spoke she laid her hand for a moment upon my arm, as though to satisfy herself that I was really made of human flesh and blood, and not a phantom standing beside her in the starlit darkness.

Scarce knowing what I did, I laid my own hand, warm and strong and firm, upon hers. For an instant I felt it tremble beneath mine. I would have given all the boundless wealth that I knew was mine for the courage to close upon it a grasp that it could not have escaped if it would. My heart seemed to swell as though it would burst in my breast, my tingling blood ran fire, and wild words rose choking to my lips. Then her hand slipped away from under mine. Once more I saw her eyes shine in the starlight, and then I knew that I had learned the last and greatest lesson that Joyful Star could teach me.

I knew now why to think of Golden Star as

my wife and my queen, filled me with the same untold horror which I had heard that night thrill in the tones of her who stood beside me, for now I—the son of a lost race and a long-past age—loved this daughter of the new time. For good or evil, for hope or despair, I was hers until I went again, and for the last time, into the shadows through which I had already passed, and then—yes, there he was, this tall, stalwart, golden-haired son of her own race and her own time, whose eyes I had seen looking love into hers!

He was coming towards us round the lake with his long, easy, swinging strides, this man who was already my friend, and who would one day be the captain of my armies. For one blind moment of madness I thought how completely I had him and the others in my power; of the lonely, unknown valley where we stood; of the men who were already my slaves, and who looked upon me as a god. I thought, too, of the dark, deep waters of the lake, and the secrets that they held for me alone. How well they could hide others for me, too! What if Golden Star never awoke? Would she not be as well lying there in the peace of her endless sleep as coming back into the world, perhaps to love in vain and to suffer as I was doomed to suffer?

The shadowy forms of the mountains began

to waver and reel around me; the stars danced up and down in the sky, and a red mist seemed to swim before my eyes. Then, through the hoarse, dull murmur that was sounding in my ears, I heard the sweet, low voice of Joyful Star saying,—

'Ah, Captain Hartness, I suppose you have been wondering what had become of us! I am afraid I have been neglecting my household duties, and you have been attending to them for me, but really I could not resist coming here with Vilcaroya. Look, that is where Golden Star is lying, in a cave under that great rock down there where those dark shadows are. Doesn't it look cold and lonely and eerie?'

'Yes,' he answered, with a laugh that did not sound to me like his own. 'But I don't suppose that matters very much now to Her Highness any more than it did to Vilcaroya. But, to descend to less romantic matters, I have come to tell you that the affairs of our temporary household are already in order, supper is ready, and we are all ravenously hungry, and I suppose you are about the same. This mountain air puts an edge on one's appetite like a razor's.'

'Supper—yes, I had forgotten all about it, thinking of poor Golden Star lying there all alone in the darkness. Of course, I am desperately hungry, now that you remind me of it. Come, Vilcaroya, I am sure you are hungry too. Another night alone won't matter much to poor Golden Star after all these years. You can dream of her to-night, as I suppose we all shall, and to-morrow we shall see her. Oh, how I wonder what she will be really like!'

As Joyful Star said this in a voice that was half sad and half merry, she turned away towards Francis Hartness, and I followed her with some light words on my lips and many heavy thoughts in my heart, and we walked together to the tents, talking of the things that were to be done on the morrow.

The next morning I was afoot before the stars had begun to pale in the coming dawn. I had not slept for two hours together through the night, yet, waking and sleeping, many dreams had come to me. I had been back to the past among my people, living again that strange old life, with all its light and colour and gaiety, which was now every day becoming more and more like a vision that had been told to me by some other dreamer.

I had talked with Golden Star, seeking to teach her the lesson that my dear instructress of the new time had taught me, and had awakened half mad with the perplexities of my divided love—the love of the past that was dead and of the present that was alive. I had seen my sister-bride come forth out of her tomb to greet me, clothed in her bridal robes, with the dust of the grave in her hair and on her face. I had clasped her in my longing arms and kissed the dust from her lips, and while I yet held her in my embrace her form had grown cold and stiff again. Then, in the agony of my sorrow, I had strained her to my breast, and, under the pressure of my arms, she had crumbled in my grasp and fallen, a little heap of grey bones and dusty garments, at my feet.

Once more I had awakened with my gasping cry of horror still sounding in my ears, and then, not daring to seek sleep again, I had risen and gone out to watch for the rest of the night before her grave under the rock. There they found me when they came from the camp at daybreak. I went back with them, and our hasty morning meal was eaten and drunk almost in silence, for we were all too busy with our thoughts to have leisure for conversation, and my friends, knowing how much that day's work must mean to me, respected my unspoken feelings, and left me to the silent company of my own hopes and fears.

Breakfast over, we took our lanterns and tools and went to the rock, followed by Tupac and two of my men carrying the coffin-like case in which Golden Star's body was to be laid. Under the rock was a long heap of loose stones which the professor had wisely piled up in front of the upright courses of masonry through which he had broken into my resting-place. He scanned them eagerly to see if they had been disturbed since his visit, and told us that they had not. Then I bade Tupac and the men clear them away, which they speedily did, laying bare the courses of stone behind them, still standing as the professor had re-built them after taking out my body.

A few minutes' more work opened a passage large enough for a man to walk in, stooping. As if by a common instinct they all stepped aside and looked at me. I saw what they meant, and, turning the light of my lantern into the entrance, I walked back, a living man, into the grave where I had lain dead while ten generations of men had lived and died. I saw the place where I had lain, for a few mouldering scraps and shreds of cloth and furs still lay where my bed had been. Then I flashed my lantern round the walls of the cavern, and on the side along which my own couch had been spread by Anda-Huillac and his brother priests I found what they had told me to seek while I was preparing to fulfil the oath that I had sworn with Golden Star.

It was a wedge of stone fitted in to a crevice in the wall and left rough and jagged at its outer end, so that one who did not know its true purpose would have taken it to be nothing more than a natural projection in the rough side of the cavern.

With a mallet that I had brought with me I struck the end of the wedge softly above and below until it was loosened in its socket. Then, standing to one side, I struck it harder. It dropped from its place, and the same instant a part of the cavern wall swayed outwards and fell with a rumbling crash across the floor.

For a moment I stood breathless and motionless on the threshold of Golden Star's grave. Then, with trembling hands, I turned the light of my lantern into the inner chamber, and as the dust that the falling stone had raised fell slowly back to the ground I saw through the particles dancing in the lantern rays the dim outline of a human form lying on a couch of skins.

Still, not daring to set a foot within that sacred place, I stood in the doorway and let the light fall full upon the figure. A glance showed me that so far all was well. No profaning hand had disturbed the peace and sanctity of her long slumber. She lay there as perfect in form and feature as she had lain beside me that night in the little chamber in the Sanctuary of the Sun.

Then I thought of Joyful Star. Hers should be the first eyes after mine to look upon that dead loveliness. So I turned and went out to where they were all standing round the outer entrance, and, taking no notice of the others, replying nothing to their half-whispered questions, I went to Ruth and, holding out my hand for her, said,—

'Come, Joyful Star, and see the sister that the

Lord of Life made long ago in the image that you now wear.'

She said nothing, but, with a look of wondering question, put her hand into mine and I turned to lead her to the entrance.

Djama, with a sudden exclamation, took a step forward as though he would stop her, but Francis Hartness put his hand on his shoulder, saying,—

'I think you had better let them go alone. There is no fear for your sister with all of us here so near; and if what Vilcaroya says is true, why should she not see her first?'

Djama drew back, though with no very good grace, and I went into the inner chamber, helping Ruth over the fallen stones. Then I flashed my light on Golden Star's face and said,—

'Did I not tell you truly that the Lord of Life made her in the same image as yours?'

I heard her utter a little gasping cry of wonder, and then I saw her slip forward on to her knees beside Golden Star's pillow, and as the light fell upon the two faces—the living and the dead—the likeness between them was so perfect, save for the golden gleam of Joyful Star's hair and the lustrous blackness of the tresses that framed my dead love's face, that they seemed to me as sisters, one watching over the slumbers of the other.

'It is more than wonderful, and it is surely more

than chance!' said Joyful Star, in a tone that was almost a whisper, and turning towards me her white face and the eyes into which the loving tears of pity were already springing. 'Why did you not tell me of this before, Vilcaroya?'

'Because,' I said, 'the arts of the priests might not have done for her what they did for me, and I might have found here that which your eyes should never have looked upon. But now—is she not beautiful, even as you are?'

The bright blood came swiftly back into her cheeks as I said this, and, without answering me she stooped, and with gentle hands put back the tresses from Golden Star's forehead, and, bending over her, laid her warm, sweet lips on the cold, smooth brow that I had last seen crowned with the marriage-garland in our bridal chamber in the Sanctuary.

CHAPTER V

HOW DJAMA DID HIS WORK

I CAN tell you but little of what followed the taking of the body of Golden Star back to the hacienda, for neither I nor any of the others, save only Djama himself, witnessed the secret mysteries of his strange and fearful art. I could tell you of their wonder when, after I had bidden Tupac bring the case into the cavern and he and I and Joyful Star had gently and reverently raised her from her couch and laid her in it, we carried her out into the daylight. How they stood around the open case and looked, half in wonder and half in fear, from her dead, cold face to the living likeness that was bending over it. How they praised her beauty and marvelled at the forgotten arts that had preserved so perfect a likeness of life in one who for more than three centuries and a half had neither drawn breath nor known a thrill of feeling.

I could tell you, too, with what loving and anxious care that precious burden was borne over plain and valley and mountain in a litter that we had brought with us for the purpose, and how at last we laid her in all her calm, unconscious loveliness on the great table which stood in the middle of the chamber in which Djama was to do his work.   But here my story must cease for the time, for Djama made it an unalterable condition that he should do the work that only he could do in absolute solitude.   Only thus, he said, would he, or could he, perform the task upon whose issue the completion of Golden Star's life on earth, if it was ever to be completed, depended.

He told us plainly that a single interruption should be fatal to her and all our hopes.   He would not even permit his sister to enter the room until he should call for her.   I was bitterly loath to yield—to leave her who had been so dear to me powerless and unconscious in the hands of a man whom I had already learned to hate, although . not only did I owe my own new life to him, but on him alone rested all my hopes of seeing Golden Star once more restored to life and health, and the beauty that had been peerless ages before Joyful Star had reached the perfection of her young womanhood.

How did I know what unholy arts he might use to rekindle the long-quenched life-flame in that fair shape of hers? How could I do more than guess vaguely and fearfully at the awful mysteries that might be enacted in the silence and solitude of that fast-closed chamber in which, day and night, he would remain alone with her, the living with the dead, like the potter with his clay, until it should please him to use the dreadful power that was his, and call her back from death to life, perhaps—and oh! how horrible the thought was to me!—to be the slave of the man who, by his unearthly art, had made himself the master of her new life.

Yet, think of it, brood over it as I would, there was no help for it. He, and he alone, could exert the power that would loose the bonds of death in which she lay enchained. Unless he had his will she would remain as she was, perhaps until the Last Day came, and the Lord of Life called all his children, living and dead, back to the Mansions of the Sun; and so we yielded, since there was nothing else to be done.

On the evening of the day that we returned to the hacienda, he busied himself making the last preparations for his work. Then he came out of the room and locked the door, and, after eating his dinner almost in silence, went to bed, taking the key with him, and telling us that on no account must he be awakened. All that night and the next day and the next night we neither saw nor heard anything of him ; but on the morning of the second day, the door of his bedroom was open and his bed was empty, but the door of the room in which Golden Star lay was still fast shut and locked.

How the time passed I cannot tell you. Joyful Star, seemingly more self-possessed than any of us, took up her household duties, and went about them with a quick, quiet industry that surprised and shamed us. But we three men wandered about aimlessly, now alone and now together, communing with our own thoughts or talking with each other always of the same thing — of what was going on in that chamber, where, as we knew from the faint sounds that every now and then came through the closed door, the master of the arts of life and death was performing his awful task.

The first day and night came and went, then the second, and still the door remained closed, and Djama gave no sign. But the professor sought to comfort me and soothe our impatience by telling me how long the same work had lasted before I was recalled to life. I had sought also to distract my thoughts by talking with him and Francis Hartness of all that was to be done for the deliverance of my people, and the realisation of my dreams of empire when Djama's task should be over.

But it was useless, for fear and suspense kept my mind bound as though with invisible chains, and, do what I would, my thoughts went back and back again to dwell upon the unknown secrets of that closed and silent room. Then I tried to draw Joyful Star into conversation about the thoughts which I knew were filling both our hearts; but though she listened to me she would say nothing herself, and I soon saw that with her the subject was forbidden, and the work not to be talked of till, in success or failure, it was ended.

For the first two nights no sleep came to my eyes, but the third night my weariness was too much for me, and scarcely had my aching head fallen on the pillow than slumber, filled with broken dreams and visions of things unutterably horrible, came upon me. In the midst of one of them—I know not what it was, save that no human words could paint the horror of it—I woke up with a cold, damp hand upon my shoulder, and heard Djama's voice, hoarse and trembling, saying to me,—

'Get up and dress, Vilcaroya; I have something for you to see and to hear. Make haste, for there is not much time to be lost.'

I looked up, and saw him standing by my bed with a light in his hand, ghastly pale, and staring at me with black, burning eyes, which seemed, as they looked into mine, to take my will a prisoner, and draw my very soul towards him.

'What is it?' I said, in the broken words of one just roused from sleep. 'Is it over—have you succeeded? Is she alive? Have you come to take me to her?'

'The work is not done yet,' he said. 'I have come for you to see it finished. Make haste, I tell you, if you want to see what you have been waiting so long for.'

I needed no second bidding. I sprang out of bed, and dressed myself with swift, though trembling, hands. Then I thrust my feet into a pair of soft slippers, such as Djama himself wore, and then I followed him from the room out on to the balcony that was built round the house over the inner courtyard. We went down into the court and into the dining-room, and through that down a long, narrow passage out of which opened the room that had held all our hope and fear and wonder for so long.

He unlocked the door, and motioned to me to go in. He followed me, and locked the door behind us. I looked about the room, which was dimly lit by two shaded lamps. The table on which we had laid Golden Star was empty. Many strangely-shaped things, that I knew not the use of were scattered about. The air was hot and moist, and filled with a faint, sweet odour. At the opposite end from the door, which was covered by a screen, I saw in one corner a bath—from which white, steamy fumes were rising—and in the other stood a little, narrow, curtained bed, such as I had first awakened in.

Djama caught me by the arm, and half led, half dragged me to the bedside. Then with his other hand he parted the curtains and pointed to the pillow. I felt his burning eyes fixed upon me as I looked and saw the sweet fair face of Golden Star lying in the midst of her dusky tresses, which lay spread out on the pillow, cleansed from the dust of the grave, and soft and shimmering as silk.

I started forward, and, with my face close to hers, scanned every feature, and listened, but in vain, for the soft sound of her breathing. Her skin was clear and moist; I could see the thin, blue veins in her eyelids, and the moisture on her lips. I laid my hand gently on her cheek. It was soft and smooth, but still cold as death.

Then a fierce, unreasoning anger came into my heart. I sprang back and seized Djama by the shoulders, and, looking with fierce, hot eyes into his, I whispered hoarsely,—

'Have you brought me here to mock me? She is not alive—she is but a fair image of death. Tell me that you have failed and I will strangle you, liar and cheat that you are!'

He looked back steadily into my eyes and smiled, and said, in a voice that had not the slightest tremor of fear,—

'If I fail you may strangle me, and welcome; but I have not failed yet, Vilcaroya. It is for *you* to say now whether Golden Star is to awake or not.'

'What do you mean?' I said, letting go my grip on his shoulders, and recoiling a pace from him.

'You shall hear what I mean,' he said. 'But you must hear patiently and quietly, and think well on what I say, for in your answer to what I ask you will also answer the question whether Golden Star is to awake to life and health, or to be put back in that case yonder and buried, to rot away into corruption like any other corpse.'

'Say on, I am listening,' I said. My lips were dry, and the grip of a deadly fear seemed to be clutching at my heart and draining the last drop of blood from it.

'Listen well, then,' he said. He paused for a moment as though to collect his thoughts, and make words ready to express them. Then he went on. 'You see, I have undone the work that your priests did three hundred and sixty years ago. Your Golden Star is now neither dead nor alive. She is lying on the narrow borderland that divides life from death, and for an hour from the time I left this room she will remain there—if I choose. At the end of that time she will pass beyond the border, and no earthly power, not even mine, could call her back. But at any time before the hour has expired I can complete the work that I have begun. I can bring the breath back to her body; I can set the blood flowing through her veins. You shall see her eyes open and her lips smile, and you shall hear her speak to you as though she had only awakened out of sleep. This I can do, and I will, if you will do what I am going to ask you.'

'What is it?' I whispered. 'Tell me quickly that I may know. You are master here. I can only listen and obey.'

He smiled as I said this, a smile that it was not good for an honest man to look upon, and went on, speaking now rapidly and earnestly,—

'When I did this work for you, I did it as a student and a man of science, who was making the greatest experiment of his life. I believed that I had solved one, at least, of the secrets of life and death. I watched and noted every change that came over you. I marked every symptom and measured every step of your return from death into life, but I did all this as a student inquiring into the mysteries of Nature, as an observer watching the working out of a great problem, and with no more feeling than if I had been dissecting a corpse. But this time it has been different. I began this work with the cold and passionless deliberation of one who toils only to learn and to succeed. But afterwards—come here and look at her, and you will understand me better. She is a woman, and she is beautiful, and here, for two days and two nights, she has lain under my hands and my eyes. I have given her beauty back to her, and if that beauty is to live it must be mine. Do you understand me, Vilcaroya?'

What could I say, what could I do to answer this man whom I hated, and yet who held the power of life and death for Golden Star in his hands? The vague fear that had smitten me when he began to speak had taken its worst shape now. I looked at him with hate and horror staring out of my eyes. Again and again I tried to speak, but my lips only moved and trembled without making any word. But he read my thoughts, and smiled that evil smile of his again and said, in a low voice which seemed to have the echo of a laugh in it,—

'I see you hate me, as I have often thought you did, and that is why I have brought you here to tell you this. That is why I would not complete my work till you had sworn, as you yet shall do if you would see Golden Star alive again, that what I have brought back out of the grave shall be mine and mine only.'

These last words of his let loose my anger and unchained my tongue. I gripped him by the arm, and in a whisper that had a strange hissing sound, I said,—

' But that is *not* all ! What do you think your life would be worth if you left her to die ? Have you forgotten what I said to you in the cave beneath the Rodadero ? Do you not know that this very night I could have you carried, gagged and bound, over the mountains and back to the grave that we took Golden Star out of? Do you not know that I could lay you there with food and drink beside you that you could not touch, and a lamp whose light would show them to you, and then wall up the entrance again, and leave you there to think of your fate till you went mad and died of hunger and thirst ? Do you not know that I could chain you to a rock and light a fire about you, and watch you burn limb by limb till you shrieked your life out in lingering agony ? Would this be better than going back to your own land loaded with treasure that would make you richer than you have ever dreamed of being? Now, *I* have spoken, and it is for you to answer me.'

Before I had done speaking he had taken a chair and seated himself astride it, with his arms resting on the back and his chin on his arms, and was looking at me with white, set face, and steady, dark, shining eyes. When I had finished there was a little silence between us, and then he spoke, and the first time I ever felt fear in either of my lives was when I heard those cold, cruel, carefully-measured words of his,—

'That is well said, Vilcaroya. I am glad you have spoken plainly, for now we understand each other; but I don't think you quite realise the difference between your power and mine. You have, or think you have, the brute force, the strength of numbers, and the slavish devotion of your people on your side, and you threaten to use that power to put me to a lingering and torturing death unless I withdraw my demands and do as you wish me. In that, however, you are quite wrong. I am as much the master of my own life as I was once of yours, and still am of Golden Star's. Without moving hand or foot I could kill myself as I sit here before you, so your threats of torture are nothing more than empty words. It is only a matter of simple life or death. If I live, Golden Star will live. If I die, she will never draw the breath of life—but what I have said, I have said. She shall only live as my promised wife, bound to me by the most sacred oath that you can swear. You cannot consummate your own marriage with her, because in the modern world that is impossible.

You are refusing simply because, for some reason
or other, you dislike me personally, but I don't
propose that that shall stand in my way.   As
for your treasures, their value has utterly changed
for me.   A week ago, I frankly confess that I
would have sold my soul, if I thought I had one,
for them.   Now, without her, they would only
make the world a golden mockery to me, for I
tell you, Vilcaroya, that I, who have never loved
living woman yet, love that beautiful shape of
inanimate flesh as that old sculptor we have told
you of loved his statue.   Every hour that I have
been alone in this room with her this strange
love of mine has grown.   First it was only scientific curiosity, then physical admiration, then
something else.   I don't know what it is, for it
is beyond the reach of my analysis, but I know
enough of it to call it love, and I tell you it is
such love as only a man of my nature and pur-
suits is capable of.   Unsatisfied, it would consume
me and kill me, and I would rather die quickly
than slowly.   Now—once more—shall Golden
Star and I live or die?'

How was I to answer such a speech as this?
I heard him in silence to the end, my eyes held
fast by his, and my spirit sinking as though
beaten down by the pitiless force of those cold
words of his.   And in the meantime a great
truth had been dawning in my mind.   Force

had ceased to rule in this new world, and intellect had taken its throne. I was the inferior
of this man, whose trained mind was the heir
of the generations that had toiled and fought
while I had slept. I was little better than a
savage before him, and I knew it, and he knew
it, and, bitter as the thought was to me, yet it
was only the truth. I was conquered, and
a new gleam in his eyes told me that he
had read my thoughts before I had spoken
them.

Then, while I stood hesitating before him, his
white, hard-set face softened, and his lips melted
into a smile that was almost as sweet as a
woman's. It was that that saved me, for it re-
minded me of Ruth, and the recollection of her
told me that I loved even as Djama did. The
very thought of her put new blood into my
heart. The words of yielding and submission
died unuttered on my lips. I raised my head,
which I had bowed down in dejection, and
looked at him steadily again. Then I said
slowly, and in the voice of a man who does not
speak twice,—

'I have thought, and I will speak for the last
time. I will swear by the sacred glory of the
Lord of Light that Golden Star shall be yours,
upon two conditions.'

'Conditions!' said he, bringing his dark brows

The dagger-point dropped till it was within an inch of Golden Star's breast.

To face page 119.

down till they made a straight black line over his eyes. 'What are they?'

'These,' I said. 'You love and I love. First, then, you must win the love of Golden Star, and, secondly, you must give me your sister, Joyful Star, if I can win her love.'

'My sister Ruth to *you!* Is that your earnest, Vilcaroya, or are you only trying my patience?'

The bitter, coldly-spoken words cut into my soul as the lash of a whip cuts into the flesh. I could have slain him as he sat there sneering at me, but it was a time for words, not deeds; and so, mastering my anger as best I could, I took two swift strides to Golden Star's bedside, and, snatching my dagger out of the sheath of the belt which I had put on when I had dressed, I turned and faced him, and said,—

'I am not jesting. As you love I love, and by the glory and majesty of my Father the Sun I tell you if you do not say yes I will do with this dagger what all your art will never repair, and then, if I must do that, I will kill you too; and before to-morrow night has passed Joyful Star shall be with me where none can find her. Now, what is your answer—yes, or no?'

He looked at me and then at the dagger hanging in my hand, point downwards, over the breast of Golden Star. Then his eyes fell upon the still loveliness of her face. He knew that if he moved the dagger would fall. His face, flushed a moment before, grew grey and pale again at the sound of my words, and then I saw that he had not lied to me when he said that his life would be worthless without her. Twice, thrice, his lips moved without shaping a word. Then the words came. They were dry and broken and trembling, for in the strength of my own love I had now conquered my conqueror, and he said,—

'Yes, since it must be so. My sister for your sister. Well, I suppose it's a fair exchange. We hate each other, you and I, but that's an accident of fate. Take away your dagger. I know when I am beaten, and I am beaten now. Will you swear that oath of yours again?'

'Yes,' I said, 'and you?'

I still kept the dagger within a span of Golden Star's heart, for I still had but little trust in his faith. He rose from his chair, throwing it over as he did so, and stood up and faced me, saying,—

'There is no need for oaths either from you or me. We have both too much to lose to break faith. Put up your dagger and come away, and in ten minutes from now you shall hear Golden Star draw the first breath of her new life, and see her eyes open and look at you. That would be worth more than any oath I could swear, wouldn't it?'

'Yes,' I said, 'but that is not all or enough. If

you broke faith with me after that, I should have to shed blood—my sister's and yours. Now I need only make her life impossible. I will stop here. Go you and wake your sister and bring her here. Then we will say more.'

'Bring Ruth here!' he cried, staring at me as though he wished, as no doubt he did, that the fierce light in his eyes could blast and wither me where I stood. 'Bring her here to see what no human eyes but mine have ever seen. Bring her here to listen to what you have said—and if her, why not Lamson and Hartness as well?'

'You may bring all, if you please,' I said, 'but Joyful Star must come, no matter what she hears or sees. I have spoken—now go, or Golden Star shall never wake again.'

He took a half pace towards me, with clenched hands and set teeth, crouching like a mountain lion about to spring on its prey. The dagger point dropped till it was only an inch from Golden Star's breast. If he had made another step I would have driven it home. He read in my eyes that I would do so, and he stopped. Then he hissed a curse at me through his clenched teeth, and turned and walked away towards the door. As he reached it he looked back, and saw me still standing there with the dagger ready to do the work that could never be undone. I saw his lips move, but heard no sound.

Then he unlocked the door, went out, and locked it after him, leaving me there alone with my dead sister-love, whose new life, with all its possibilities of love and happiness, or hate and misery, I had thrown into the balance of Fate in the game that I was playing against him to win that other love which had now become tenfold more dear to me.

When he had gone I took his chair and put it by the side of the bed and sat down, still holding my bare dagger in my hand and looking on Golden Star's dead loveliness, wondering what it would be like when the sunshine of her new life should shine upon it, and on whom her first glance would fall, or whose name be the first that her lips would speak, and as I sat and watched and waited it seemed to me as though the ghosts of those long dead were taking shape and ranging themselves about the bed of her re-awakening as they had done about the bed of her falling asleep and mine.

I saw Anda-Huillac and his brother priests of the Sun standing about me, gazing at me and at her with sad and dreamy eyes, like phantoms of the past looking upon the realities of the present. Then the shape of Anda-Huillac seemed to glide towards me. His ghostly eyes looked into mine, and a smile of pity and reproach moved his pale lips. I felt a cold, soft hand laid upon mine, my grasp relaxed and the dagger fell ringing to the floor.

The sound awoke me, and my vision vanished. How long it had lasted, or whether it was a vision of sleep or waking, I know not, but I was awake now for I heard the door creek on its hinges. I picked the dagger up again and started to my feet, and, still guarding Golden Star's bed, I turned and faced Djama as he came in, followed by the professor and Francis Hartness, with Joyful Star between them.

CHAPTER VI

THE WAKING OF GOLDEN STAR

'THERE is your royal, would-be lover, Ruth! Come, if you don't believe me, you can hear from his own lips that upon you, and you alone, depends Golden Star's return to life. Is not that so, Your Highness?'

It was Djama who said this, and as he said it, he caught Joyful Star by the hand and half led, half dragged her towards me from between the other two. But before he had come half the length of the room, Francis Hartness had overtaken him in a few swift strides. I saw his hand fall heavily on his shoulder, and with his other hand he took Ruth's out of his. His blue eyes were nearly black with anger, and his bronzed face was grey and set and pale with the passion that his strong will was holding back, and his voice was low and clear, and vibrating like the sound of a distant bell when he spoke and said,—

'I can't stand that, Djama. Are you forgetting that your sister is a woman, and that you have brought her into the presence of the dead?'

'You must be mad, Laurens!' said Joyful Star, before her brother could reply. 'Surely this dreadful work of yours has turned your brain. Vilcaroya, what does all this mean? Is Golden Star dead or alive? Ah, how beautiful she is now! No, surely she cannot be dead!'

She had broken away from both her brother and Francis Hartness, and as she said the last words she was leaning over Golden Star's pillow, softly stroking her hair; and then she stooped lower and kissed her forehead. Then the others came up to the bedside, Francis Hartness and Djama in front, and the professor standing silent and wondering behind them.

'If Djama won't speak, will you, Vilcaroya?' said Hartness, looking at me with eyes that were still angry. 'What is that dagger in your hand for, and what is the meaning of this story that he has been telling me?'

'The meaning is of life or death,' I said. 'Laurens Djama will not give Golden Star's life back to her if I will not swear to give her to him when she lives again, and I have sworn that he shall not restore her to life unless he swears to give Joyful Star to me, for I love her, and will have neither life nor empire without her.'

As I listened to my own voice saying these bold words, it seemed to me as though another were speaking, for, even in that hot moment of passion and desperate resolve, I could scarce believe them mine. For the instant, I thought Hartness would have struck me down where I stood, nor could I have used my dagger against him, for he was a man and I loved him, though I saw now that we both loved the same woman. But before either of us could move, Ruth had risen erect and come between us, her cheeks burning with shame and her eyes aglow with anger.

'What!' she said, 'Laurens give me to you, Vilcaroya! Don't you know yet that no one can give an English girl away except herself, and that she only gives herself to the man she chooses of her own free will? Do you think I am a slave or a human chattel to be bartered away like that? Nonsense! And you, Captain Hartness, don't look so fiercely at Vilcaroya. Remember that he is your friend and mine, or has been, and has not the same ideas as we have. If he had—'

'He has,' I said, breaking in upon her speech, 'since Joyful Star has spoken. He is not her lover but her slave, and she has shamed him.

I will eat the words that should never have been spoken. Let Golden Star live! I will keep my oath and ask nothing in return.'

So the savage within me was tamed, and I, who but a few minutes before had been ready to take two lives at the prompting of a single word, dropped my dagger and stood with bowed head, humble as a chidden child before her whose lightest word was then my most sacred law. I raised my eyes and looked at her to see if my words had pleased her. As our eyes met she gave me a glance that I would have died to win from her, and then, pushing me and Francis Hartness gently aside, yet with a force that neither of us could have resisted, she took her brother by the arm and, leading him to the bedside with one hand, she laid the other on Golden Star's brow, and said,—

'Laurens, can you really bring her back to life?'

'Yes,' he answered, and I could see that he did not dare to raise his eyes to hers, 'but—'

'But you will only do it for a price, you think. For shame! Is that the way you would use this terrible power that you possess? Is my brother so mean a creature as that? You love her, you say, even as she lies there, neither dead nor alive? Well, when she lives, she will be worthy of any man's love, but only of a man's, Laurens, and you would not be a man, with all your learning and power, if you insisted on so mean an advantage as your skill gives you. Do you mean to tell me that you can look on such a beauty as that, knowing that you can restore it to life, and yet ask a price before you will do it ? Come, Laurens, that is not like your old self. Use your power with the same generosity that it has been given to you, and then win Golden Star like a man if you can.'

Where my strength had been vanquished, her sweet wisdom conquered. The man who had laughed at my threats, and told me without a quiver in his voice how he could, and would, slay himself rather than I should do what he knew I could do, stood humbled and abashed before the righteous and yet gently-spoken reproach of her who was pleading for the life of a sister woman.

I saw Djama's hands meet behind his back, and his fingers begin to twine about each other. I saw him look from Ruth to Golden Star, from the living woman who was his sister to her lifeless counterpart. Then came over him one of those swift changes of mood which we had so often seen before. All the cold cruelty of his long-chained-up passion vanished. His face, from being stone, became flesh again. The fierce glitter, as of a sword's point, died out of his eyes, and they grew warm and soft again, and his voice was almost as sweet and gentle as Ruth's, and strangely like it, too, as he answered her and said,—

'You are right, Ruth. I was not myself. I was a brute, unworthy either of love or power. Let her die! Good God, I would die myself a thousand times rather than do that! I must have been out of my senses even to think of such a crime for a moment, but if you were a man and had lived through what I have lived through for the last two days and nights, you would understand me, and perhaps forgive me. Yes, she shall live. How could I ever have thought of letting her die!'

Then he rose from his half-stooping posture over the bed, and came to where I stood at the foot, and, with his hand outstretched and a smile on his lips, said,—

'You have heard what I have just said, Vilcaroya. You have withdrawn your conditions; now I will take back mine. It is no use for you and me to be enemies. We have had our fight, and I confess myself beaten. Now let us try to be friends for Ruth's sake and Golden Star's, and I promise you that to-morrow morning you shall be telling her the story of your resurrection and her own.'

For a moment I stared at him in, speechless wonder, striving to understand how it could be that those eyes, which had, but a short time before, been glaring hate at me, could now be looking so kindly and frankly into mine; and how those lips, which had just been sneering so coldly and cruelly alike at my love and my hate, could shape such friendly and honest-sounding words. Then I looked at Ruth, asking her with my eyes what she would have me do, and in instant obedience to what I saw took Djama's hand in mine and said,—

'So be it! The evil in our hearts has spoken, now let the good that is there speak, and let us be friends; and, when Golden Star awakes, with my lips she shall bless you and her who has made peace between us where there was strife.'

'Miss Ruth, you really must allow me to congratulate you on your success as a peace-maker,' said the professor, speaking now for the first time since he had come into the room, and coming forward to where Joyful Star still stood by the bedside. 'It would have been ten thousand pities if this—ah—this little affair had ended any other way, for all of the exquisitely perfect subjects—'

'*Subjects*, professor?' said Ruth, interrupting him with a laugh. 'Do you venture to call Golden Star a subject, just as you do those awful things in your dissecting-rooms? Look at her—a *subject* indeed! Don't call her that again in my hearing, please!'

'Oh, ah, of course, I beg your pardon a thousand times, and Her Highness's too. Really, I spoke quite thoughtlessly and most improperly.' he answered, laughing at her mock displeasure, 'And now, Djama, since we have had two declarations of love and a peacemaking, don't you think it would be cruel to keep Her Highness waiting any longer on the threshold of her new life? Come, Hartness, you and I have no more business here at present. Don't you think we had better go and wait somewhere else for the working of the miracle?'

'Just what I was going to say,' replied Hartness, who had gone away a little distance from the bed while we were talking, and had been standing by the table, seeming to examine the strange instruments that were scattered about it. 'Of course the doctor will wish to finish his work alone.'

'May not Vilcaroya and I stay, Laurens?' asked Joyful Star, looking at him with appealing eyes. 'You know it will be much better for her to see another woman by her when she awakes, and then she will recognise Vilcaroya, and that will tell her that she is among friends.'

But Djama shook his head and said,—

'No, Ruth, not yet. There is something else

to be done before that—something, well, something that only a medical man ought to sec or do, and you really must leave me to do it alone. You forget, it is not merely a matter of waking. She is not alive yet; but if you will leave me alone for about half-an-hour, I promise you that I will call you and Vilcaroya back before she actually wakes.'

'Very well,' she said, moving away from the bedside. 'I don't want to pry into your mysteries.' Then she turned to me, and said, with a faint smile on her lips, 'Vilcaroya, come into the dining-room, I have something to say to you.'

She went down the room after the professor and Francis Hartness, and I followed her with beating heart and anxious thoughts, wondering what new lesson it was she was about to teach me.

Djama closed and locked the door after us. She led the way to the dining-room, where there was a light burning. It was empty, for the others, hearing what she had said to me, had gone out into the courtyard. Then she turned and faced me with her back to the light; but in spite of that I could see that her eyes were bright, and her fair face flushed as she said to me in a low voice that trembled a little,—

'Vilcaroya, I am going to forget everything that was said in the room yonder, and—and you must forget it too. It was no time or place for such things to be said, and you and Laurens were not yourselves when you said them. If you do not forget them, we cannot be friends any more. You understand me, don't you?'

Gentle and sweetly spoken as the words were, they fell upon my heart like snow upon a fainting flame; yet I felt that, like all her words, they were true and just. I crossed my hands on my breast with one of my old-world gestures, and, standing so before her with bowed head, I said,—

'The will of Joyful Star is my law. Let what I spoke in my madness be forgotten as you have said. Who am I that I should say such things?—a poor savage that has wandered from his own world into hers, where he is a stranger!'

'No, not a savage, Vilcaroya. You must never say that word again. How could Golden Star's brother be a savage? How could I— but there, we have said enough for the present. We have other things to think of now.'

With that she turned away and sat down in a long, low chair, resting her cheek upon her hand, and looking out of one of the windows at the stars, while I went and stood before another to look at the same stars that she was looking at, and so we waited in silence until the door opened, and we heard Djama's voice telling us that the long - expected moment of Golden Star's awakening had come at last.

As Joyful Star went to the door I stood aside and waited for her to pass me and go out first. As she went by our eyes met for a moment, and I saw that hers were bright with tears. My heart leapt at the sight, and then fell still again and well nigh fainting. What had she said to me but a few minutes before? How dare I dream that those sweet tears could be for me?

I followed her and Djama into the room, but half-way between the door and the bed I stopped, not daring to go on, held back by some impulse I could not name. I saw her lean over the pillow for a moment in silence that for me was breathless. Then came a soft, sweet sound, and then a little cry. Was it her's or Golden Star's?

Djama beckoned to me. I went with swift, silent steps to the foot of the little bed, and saw Golden Star's eyes wide open and looking wonderingly up into Ruth's face, and her red lips smiling at her. The miracle had been completed. She had awakened her with a kiss.

'Come and give her your welcome back to life, Vilcaroya,' she whispered, rising and turning her fair face with its wet cheeks and smiling lips towards me. I went and stood over the pillow, and laid my trembling lips on Golden Star's brow, and then I said, in the words that had been the first of my own new life,—

'*Cori-Coyllur Ñustallipa, Ñusta mi!*'

She looked at me, but there was no more recognition in her gaze than in that of a new-born child, nor was there any answering smile upon her lips. Unheeding this for the moment, I went on and said, still speaking very gently and softly in our own tongue,—

' Thou art thrice welcome back from the shades of night into the bright presence of our Father the Sun, oh, Golden Star! Dost thou not remember me, Vilcaroya, thy brother, who went into the darkness with thee long ago, and has been permitted to return before thee that he might greet thee and bid thee welcome ?'

Her eyes wandered from my face to Joyful Star's, and then she smiled again, but no answering words came from her parted lips. Now, as we looked from one another to her, a great fear came into all our hearts, and Ruth gave it voice.

' Laurens,' she whispered, laying her hands upon his arm, ' what is the matter? Vilcaroya spoke at once, didn't he? Why doesn't she speak? Oh, surely it can't be that she is—that she has come back to life without memory or—or her reason? What is it?'

I waited for Djama's answer as a man might wait for words that were to tell him whether he was to live or die. He put us both gently away from the bed, and then, laying his hand on Golden Star's brow, he looked long and steadfastly into her eyes. It seemed to me as though Ruth and I could hear each other's hearts beating and counting off the seconds until he raised his head again and said in the slow, even tones of the man of science who, for the time, had overcome and banished the lover,—

'Memory, perhaps, even probably; but reason, no. These are not the eyes of an imbecile or an idiot, but they *are* the eyes of a child. It is possible that when she fully recovers we may find her mind a perfect blank—a virgin page on which the story of her new life will have to be written.'

'Thank God for that!' she murmured, and I, too, echoed her words in my heart, though I did not know then how much she meant by them.

Then once more she turned and went to Golden Star's pillow, laying her hand upon her brow again, and looking fondly for a moment on the silent and yet eloquent face that was looking up at her. Then she said to her brother,—

'But is she well now? I mean, is her physical

life certain? Will she live and grow well and
strong again?'

'Yes,' he answered. 'I have done everything
that it is in my power to do. I have fulfilled my
promise to His Highness. The rest is, as it was
with him, merely a matter of care and nourishment and nursing.'

'Then,' she said, with a swift, subtle change
coming over her manner, 'the care and the
nursing must be mine, and you two must say
good-bye to her for the present, until I have
nursed her back to health. Of course you may
see her when necessary, as her doctor, but only
as her doctor, mind. And you, Vilcaroya, must
possess yourself with what patience you can until
my part of the work is done as well. Now, go
away, both of you. I am mistress here for the
present. Laurens, you go and get ready the
nourishment that you think she should take, and
come back in half-an-hour, and tell me how it
is to be taken.'

It was easy for us to see the deep yet kindly
meaning of her lightly-spoken words, for in them
she had told us that Golden Star was now once
more a living woman. No longer a mummy, or
a corpse, or a 'subject,' as the professor had
called her—no longer an inanimate thing that
had neither sex nor claim to human rights—but
a sister woman of her own kind whose wants

could only be supplied by her. So we obeyed
her, and went away, leaving her there to perform
the most sacred task save one that a loving
woman could perform.

Djama went to prepare the food that Golden
Star would soon need, and I went in search of
the professor and Francis Hartness, and told
them all that had happened, and then, when
the professor had gone to bed to finish his
broken night's rest, I and he who was my rival
in love, and who was to be my brother-in-arms,
went out from the courtyard into the *patio*
which lay in front of the house, sloping down
towards the entrance of the little valley in which
the hacienda lay, and there, walking to and fro
side by side, we talked long and earnestly of
many things upon the doing of which my heart
was set, and which might now be freely entered
upon, seeing that the first object of our journey
was already achieved.

Our talk, as you may well believe, was of war
and not of love, though it would be hard to say
which of the two at that hour most filled our
secret thoughts; but, as I have told you, this
English soldier was a true man, and I trusted
him, knowing well that though, when the
imperial Llautu once more encircled my brows,
I might find courage to seek openly the love of
her into whose eyes I had already seen him

look with love, yet no falsehood or hatred could ever come between us. So I told him freely of the treasures that I had only to take from their hiding-places to make them mine, and spoke once more of the use that I would make of them, and took his advice as to the best method of that use.

This he was well able to give me, for I soon found that since he had resolved to throw in his lot with us, he had applied himself diligently to the task of studying the work that was to be ours, and seeking the best and readiest means of doing it. In Lima and Arequipa he had bought books and papers from which he had learned, as far as could be learned, the resources and power of the government of Peru, the number of its soldiers and their stations, the names and characters of the men who made the government, and of those who were opposed to them, seeking, as he told me was now ever the case in the countries of South America, to overturn the government and to take for themselves the honours and the profits of rule.

He told me—which events soon proved to be the truth—that not many months would pass by before civil war once more broke out. The President and the ministers, who were the tools of his tyranny, had oppressed the people with grievous burdens till they could endure them no longer, and already people in the towns of the interior were refusing to pay taxes, and were arming themselves in secret and meeting in bands among the mountains to practise themselves with their weapons, and make ready for the war which was so soon to come.

All this, as he soon showed me, was happening as though the Fates which rule the world had especially prepared it for my coming. The people had no leader save a man who had been himself a tyrant before, and none trusted him, but looked to him only to serve their own ends. Those who had the power were hated, and those who sought to seize it were distrusted.

But better than all was the utter, and, as far as all men, save ourselves, could see, the hopeless poverty of the country. Long years of plundering had emptied the treasury. Commerce was leaving the shores, and industries were languishing throughout the land. No man trusted his neighbour, for nearly all were in debt, and none could get paid, and my own people, the slaves of the children of the Spaniards, and the sport of their blind and brutal jesting, had borne their heavy burdens till their backs were sore, sore as their patient hearts were, and they would bear them no longer.

From the country which is called Ecuador, and which in my other life had been Quito,

the kingdom of Atahuallpa, to the southern
confines of Bolivia, which had once been part
of the Land of the Four Regions, the dominions
of my own father, all were ready to throw down
their long-borne burdens and turn and rend their
oppressors and those whose fathers had robbed
them of the land that had once been theirs.

I well remember the very words in which
Francis Hartness told me all this at much
greater length than I have set it down here;
and this is what he said when, as the stars were
paling in the sky above us and the eastern
mountains were beginning to stand out sharply
against the growing light of the coming dawn,
our long talk drew to its close,—

'In short, Vilcaroya, if I were given to that
sort of thing, I could believe that the very Fates
themselves had conspired to prepare the way
for you. You have come back to the world
and to your own country at the very moment
that these miserable wretches are getting ready
to tear each other to pieces. The government
is as hopeless as it is impossible, and the popular
party, as they call themselves, have neither a
leader that they can trust, nor money to buy
weapons and pay their soldiers with. The
treasury is empty, for, so to speak, almost
the last dollar had been stolen. The native
troops have had no regular pay for months, and

I believe they would desert to a regiment if they once believed that you are what you are, and that you possess, as you do, the means of paying them well and honestly for their help.

'And, after all, I don't know that even I, as a soldier, could call it desertion under such circumstances. You are of their own blood, the son of one of their ancient kings. These people, these Peruvians, are only mongrel descendants of those who have plundered and oppressed them for centuries. They owe them no allegiance that is worth the name; but you they would hail, not only as their lawful king, but almost as a god—as, indeed, they could well be pardoned for doing, seeing what a marvellous fate yours has been.

'The only thing to do at present, and the only thing in which I see any difficulty, is to get into communication with them in such a way that they shall come to know you without the authorities knowing anything about you or your treasures. If that could be done, I think all the rest would be easy, and then I believe that the moment you raised the flag of the old Incas, they would flock to it in thousands, and after that it would only be a matter of military management and leadership.'

'And if I will charge myself with that, my friend,' I said, as he paused for a moment; 'if I will promise you that before six more suns have risen and set, the news of my coming shall be spread far and wide through the land, and yet in such a manner that none but the faithful, the Children of the Blood themselves, shall know anything that could work us harm, will you give me the help of your skill and your knowledge of the arts of this new warfare which is so strange to me? Will you lead my armies to battle against the oppressors of my people? Will you help me to free this land of my fathers from the yoke of its tyrants, and be the war-chieftain of my people, and stand by my throne in the days when the Rainbow Banner shall once more float over the battlements of the Sacsahuaman and the City of the Sun? If you will, you shall have riches and power and all that the heart of man can desire.'

'Not all, I am afraid, Vilcaroya!' he said, interrupting me with a laugh that had but little mirth in it. 'Not all; but that would not be in your hands to give. Never mind, it is the fortune of war, or perhaps I should rather say of love. But for the rest, yes. I believe your cause is a just and righteous one, and what I can do to help it I will. Henceforth we are brothers-in-arms, even though we may perhaps be rivals in love. There, you have my hand upon it, and with it the word of an Englishman who never broke his word yet to man or woman.'

How shall I tell you of the great joy with which

those brave, honest-spoken words of his filled me?
He, the man whom I had feared most, even as I
had learned to love him most, was the first to bid
me hope—and hope I did now, in spite of all things.
So, saying nothing, for my heart was too full for
speech, I put my hand in his, and there, as the
dawn brightened over the mountains, we clasped
hands in silence and sealed our compact, and when
the sun rose swiftly over the now glittering peaks,
I let go his hand and bowed myself before it, greeting it as the bringer of a new day which was to end
the long night that had fallen over my land and my
people when the light of my last life was quenched
in the darkness of my death-sleep.

CHAPTER VII

IN THE THRONE-ROOM OF YUPANQUI

WE saw nothing of Golden Star the next day,
nor yet for many days afterwards, for, in spite
of our impatience, Ruth would not permit us to
do so. What her brother had said had speedily
proved itself to be true. She had come back to
life a child-woman. Her body was that of a girl
of seventeen years—which was her age when she
and I had drunk the draught of the death-sleep
together—and the kindly Powers that had pre-
sided over her birth had shaped her in a mould
of almost perfect womanly beauty, yet, as Djama
had said, her mind was a virgin page, from which
the story of her past life had been utterly erased,
and on whose blank whiteness the story of her
new life had yet to be written.

Now, on the writing of the first words of this
story, as Joyful Star told us in her sweetly-
serious way the night that she had sunk into

K

her first natural slumber, everything might depend.

'It is a task,' she had said that night, 'which I fear terribly to enter upon, and yet I know that I am the only one here who ought to undertake it. She will need weeks and months of most careful watching, and the sympathy that only another woman, and one who loves her as I have already learned to do, could give her. No woman ever had such a task before, and very few have had so good a work to do. There is something, too'—and here I remember how subtle a change came into her voice as she said this—'there is something in this wonderful resemblance between us which tells me that this is my duty, and I am going to devote myself absolutely to it during every hour of her waking life until she is able to do without my care. I must watch her and care for her as a mother does for her child, and you must let me do it alone as long as I wish to, just as we had to let Laurens do *his* work alone. Don't you think I am right, professor?'

'Yes,' he answered, 'perfectly right, Miss Ruth. I am sure everybody will agree with me that Her Highness could not be in better hands than yours. Indeed, as you say, yours are the only hands in which she could possibly be trusted with safety to her newly-awakening reason at such an extraordinary juncture in her life.'

To this we all agreed willingly enough, and so Joyful Star had the big room cleared out and installed herself there with all the comforts and luxuries that the inexhaustible wealth which was now at my command could provide her with, so that Golden Star should find her new world as beautiful as might be. Meanwhile the professor, with a trusty guide that I had provided him with from among my own people, plunged afresh into his beloved studies with such ardour that he seemed to have almost forgotten all else that had brought us to Peru.

Francis Hartness had gone with Tupac—who, in the sight of the Spaniards, was only his Indian servant and guide—on a mission of importance to the South, where the first rumblings of the coming war-storm were already making themselves heard. As for Djama, who, as you know, had no more interest in the work that now lay before Francis Hartness and myself than the professor had, he went about for some days gloomy and silent, and seemingly ill at ease, like a man who for a time has lost his interest in life ; and at last—it was on the twentieth day after Golden Star had awakened —he came to me when I was alone in my room and said abruptly,—

'Vilcaroya, do you think I have fairly earned my reward for what I have done ? '

'Yes,' I said, looking into his eyes and reading,

though he knew it not, the thoughts that were moving in his mind. 'You have done all that you promised to do, but we have yet said nothing of the price. How much do you ask for?'

'As much as I can get!' he said, with a laugh that pleased me but little. 'But, of course, I know the work that you yourself have come here to do, and I see that it will be expensive, so you will find me reasonable.'

'And you, I hope, will not find me ungenerous. Do you remember what you saw in the Hall of Gold?' As I said this, his self-command left him for an instant. I saw his hands close, and his lips tremble, and the fierce fire of the gold-lust spring into his eyes as he replied,—

'Yes; how could I forget it?'

'And do you remember, too,' I said, 'the words that you heard me speak when I stood before the pyramid?'

'Yes,' he replied, with a faint flush coming into his pale cheeks. 'It is not likely that I should forget them either. Why do you ask?'

'Because,' I said, speaking slowly as a man who weighs his words well, 'saving only the sacred emblems of the Sun, which it is not lawful for me to give away, all that you saw there shall belong to you and to him who made it possible for you to do what you have done. You will share it as you please—that is no care of mine—

but I have conditions to make for my own sake and that of my people.'

'What are they?' and as he spoke the flush died out of his cheeks again.

'That you shall both swear solemnly to me that, come what may, no man shall ever know from you where the gold came from, and that, more-over, you shall never utter any word of my story or Golden Star's where mortal ears can hear it, nor give any sign or word to any man or woman that shall lead him or her to guess that I am what I am, or that my work here is what it is. Swear that oath to me and you shall take your gold and go in peace.   Break it, and the fate that I told you of shall be yours.   Are you con-tent?'

'Yes,' he said, 'and more than content; and I swear to you most solemnly, on my own honour and by all that I hold sacred, that I will keep your secrets absolutely.'

'No, not here,' I said, breaking into his speech; 'and more, it is not only your oath that I want. There must be witnesses, for this is too great a thing to do lightly.   To-morrow night we will go back to the Hall of Gold, and there you shall swear your oaths and they shall be witnessed.'

'Very well,' he said.   'Whenever and where-ever you like.   But now, Vilcaroya, I have some-thing else to say to you.   Personally, you know,

I have no further interests in Peru, saving one only. Your next few years will be stormy ones, and though I believe that, with the power you have behind you, you will win in the end, yet you know as well as I do that you will have to run all the risks of a war that may be a very savage one before you succeed. You may restore the throne of the Incas, and reign upon it, or you may be killed in the first battle. You will pardon me speaking so plainly, won't you?'

I bowed my head in silence and he went on.

'In view of this, then, I am going to propose that when we leave Peru—I mean my sister and the professor and myself—you will allow Ruth to take Golden Star to England with her, say, for three years or so, in order that her education may be carried on to the best advantage. I will promise you solemnly that during that time I will not speak a word of love to her, or attempt to be anything else to her than I am to Ruth, and then if you succeed in your aims, as I hope you will, we will come back and be Your Majesty's guests for a time, and after that we shall see what more the kindly Fates may have in store for you and me.'

No man ever heard more fairly spoken or reasonable-sounding words than these were, and yet all the while I listened to them I knew that they were but used to hide the real thoughts of him who was speaking them. Yet what could I answer him? Did they not seem to point out the best of all courses that could be followed for the welfare of Golden Star and the comfort of her whose gentle hand was leading her nearer every day to the fulfilment of the promise of her new life? So, for want of anything better in my mind, I answered,—

'Your words are unwelcome to me, for so long a parting would be a great sorrow to me; yet they are wise, and that which is most pleasant is not always the best to be done.'

'Very well,' he said, 'I quite understand you, so we won't say anything more about it until then. I suppose I may tell the professor about what we are to do to-morrow night?'

'Yes,' I said; 'there will be no harm in that, since a share of the gold belongs to him as well.'

' And Hartness?'

'He knows already, for I have told him not only of the treasures in the Hall of Gold, but of many others that will be used in the work that he has sworn to do with me.'

Later on that day when the mid-day heat had cooled a little, I was walking alone in the garden of the hacienda, thinking deeply of what Djama had said and striving to find some plan of my own that would be as good and yet not make the parting that I dreaded needful. I turned, paying but little heed to my way, into a winding pathway shaded with trees and bordered with grass and flowers. I was looking down upon the ground, as was my wont, when I heard footsteps near me and looked up. I had turned the bend in the path, and there, but a few paces from me, stood Golden Star and Ruth. I started and made a motion as though I would turn back, but Ruth immediately beckoned to me smilingly, and said,—

'Come and let me introduce you to your sister, Vilcaroya. I think it's time you began to be friends again. Don't you think she is looking wonderfully well and strong, and—and beautiful ?'

You may think, but I cannot tell you, of all the feelings that rose up within me as I obeyed her invitation. It was the first time that I had seen Golden Star since the night she had awakened. Nay, was it not the first time I had seen her as a truly living woman since the night of our bridal in the Sanctuary?

She was dressed in garments made after the fashion of Ruth's own, of light grey soft stuff, and on the glorious wealth of her hair was a broad-brimmed straw hat such as Ruth wore. Indeed, to look at them both, standing there side by side, they could but have been taken for two twin sisters—daughters of the Day and Night—as my loving fancy called them afterwards—rather than the daughters of different peoples, and children of far-parted generations, whose hands, as they clasped, bridged the gulf between one age of the world and another.

As I approached, Golden Star's eyes looked at me with the simple wonder that shines out of the eyes of a little child, and like a little child she smiled at me, and then she looked at Ruth, and made a soft low sound that was almost like the cooing of a child.

'She is pleased to see you, Vilcaroya,' said Ruth, taking hold of my hand and hers, 'but of course she can't say so yet. Now, let me teach her to shake hands with you.'

Then she put into mine the soft, warm little hand that I had last clasped when we went hand in hand to the couch of our long sleep. I pressed it gently, looking at her through the tears that rose into my eyes, then I raised it to my lips and kissed it, and she smiled, and made the little soft sound again, and then Ruth put her arm around her waist and said,—

'Come, now, you are acquainted, and she likes you. This will be a most valuable lesson for her. Now, let us have a walk, and you tell me the news, if there is any.'

'Most willingly,' I said, 'for I have much news to tell.'

So we turned back along the path into the quietest part of the garden, I walking by Ruth's side. And I told her of all that had passed between her brother and me in the morning, and of what was to be done on the following night. She was looking very serious when I had finished, and I could see that many unspoken thoughts were working in her mind, and when I had done she looked up at me and said,—

'Laurens's plan seems a very good one at first sight, but of course we cannot decide upon anything until we have thought a good deal more about it, and talked it well over amongst ourselves. But, at anyrate, it would be several weeks yet before I would even think of going away with Golden Star, so there is plenty of time for that. But to-morrow night— Listen, Vilcaroya, may I ask a very great favour of you?'

'Joyful Star can ask no favour of me,' I said. 'She can speak, and I can hear and obey.'

'Nonsense, Vilcaroya! I wish you wouldn't talk like that,' she answered with pretty petulance. 'Now, suppose I was to ask you to let me see this wonderful treasure-house of yours and promise faithfully not to tell anyone about it—would you let me?'

'It is not the best that I can show you,' I

answered gladly, 'but if you desire to see it, it is yours and all that it contains. I can give your brother and the professor other gold, and I will show you a greater treasure-house than this under the Fortress itself.'

'Well,' she laughed, 'I won't say now that I won't have it, because the sight of all that gold might be too much for me, but I should dearly love to come and see it, and I think I might venture to bring Golden Star too. She's quite well and strong now, and if we are careful of her, it can't do her any harm, and it may do her good. Shall I bring her?'

'Yes,' I said, 'why not?'

At this moment we saw Djama come walking down the path towards us, and at the sight of him there came to me, like the stab of a dagger of ice, the sudden memory that, at the moment I was speaking of my treasure-house under the Sacsahuaman, I had heard a gentle rustle behind some bushes close by the path, and a sound like that of a stealthy tread.

As Djama came near to us I saw the love-light flash into his eyes, and a swift flush rise into his sallow cheeks. He held out his hand and quickened his pace, smiling as sweetly as a woman the while. I was facing him a little in advance, and I heard behind me a sharp, low, shuddering cry of terror that shook my heart as I turned to learn its cause. Golden Star had thrown her arms round Ruth's neck, and was clinging to her, trembling with fear, and looking sideways at Djama with eyes fixed and wide open with terror.

You have seen how little children will go smiling and fearless into the arms of one stranger and shrink in hate and terror from another. Their sight is keener than it is in after years, when the dust of the world's conflict has dulled it, and they can see plainly the good and the evil that is hidden behind the mask of the face. So it was with that child-soul of Golden Star's. Though I was now to her as strange as Djama, yet she had seen in me only the friend and brother who loved her and wished her well, and whose heart was clean in her sight; but in Djama she had seen at a single glance the evil that had only been revealed to me after many weeks of watching.

Though I hated him for the fear that he had caused her, yet I was glad also, for now I saw that the answer to his proposal would be easier than I had thought for. As for him, his face darkened and his black brows came together, and the love-light in his eyes changed to a glare of anger; but this was only for an instant. It passed more quickly than the thunder-clouds melt round the crest of Illampu. He stopped,

and stood with his head slightly bent and his
hands spread, palms outward, in the posture of
one who asks pardon, and said, in a voice that
had no trace of anger,—

'Forgive me, Ruth!   I am afraid I have
startled our patient—or perhaps I should rather
say yours now.   It was something more than
stupid of me to come upon you suddenly like
this, without any warning.   Of all people in the
world, I ought to have known better than that.
But I suppose seeing Vilcaroya already here
made me forget myself.   Did she start like that
when he came?'

'No,' replied Ruth, still standing with her arm
where she had thrown it around Golden Star's
shoulders, and stroking her hair with the other.
'She—she saw him farther off than you, and I
took her towards him, so I suppose the shock
was not so great.   But please go away, both of
you, now.   You see she is terribly frightened,
and she is trembling as though someone had
struck her.   I must take her into the house and
get her quiet again, or the consequences may
be serious.'

Djama turned away without a word, his face
darkening again as he did so, and with one
backward glance at Golden Star, who had now
raised her head from Ruth's breast, and was
staring after us with fixed, wide-open eyes, I

turned and walked away beside him, neither of us speaking a word, for we were both too busy with our own thoughts.

That night Francis Hartness and Tupac returned from their journey to the South, and as the professor was also in the house I told them of what I wished done on the following night, and bade Tupac make all preparation. The next day we all started in the cool of the morning to go to the Rodadero as though for a picnic, as the people of Cuzco often do, so that there might be no suspicion of our true object. We all rode upon horses, saving Golden Star, who was carried in a hammock litter, that I had had made for her, and Tupac, and six of our people who came with us as bearers and servants.

We spent the day wandering about among the huge ruins of the Sacsahuaman, and exploring the wonders of the carved rocks and underground passages and altar-places, which have been the marvel of every traveller to the hills about Cuzco, and all that I knew of the upper works I told my companions, and showed them as well as I could what the mighty fastness had been in the days of its pride and unbroken strength.

Then, when the brief twilight came, I bade one of our men take the beasts into a chamber among the rocks that I had shown him, and where plenty of fodder had been stored a few days before. After this we waited a little longer till night fell, and then I bade Tupac do what I had bidden him the day before. His voice rose shrill and plaintive in the silence, chanting a song that you may have heard the Indians singing in Peru when returning from their labours, and presently, from among the rocks on the plain, and from the shadowy lines of the Fortress, many silent figures stole out and went towards the valley in which the Sayacusca stands.

Then I told my companions that all, save those of the Blood, must have their eyes bandaged, as Djama's had been before, and when they had submitted willingly to this, knowing that no harm would come to them, we led them to the Sayacusca, I leading Ruth by the hand, and following the bearers of Golden Star's litter, and there the way to the Hall of Gold was opened as before, and we entered it, followed by a long line of the Children of the Blood.

But I made no halt here, nor did I let my companions even see the treasure that was to be divided between Djama and the professor according to my promise, for I had greater marvels in store for them. So, lantern in hand, I led the way through a winding gallery behind the pyramid of gold of which I told you before.

At the end of this was a door, formed by a revolving stone similar to that at the entrance to the hall. This Tupac and another opened under my directions, and we entered a long, straight passage behind it. At the end was a broad flight of stone steps, and at the top were two low bronze doors bolted into pillars on either side. The doors had no hinges, but they turned with the pillars, and no one who did not know this, or how the pillars turned, could open them. But this secret was one of many others that I had brought with me from the past, and in a few moments the doors were standing open before us.

We passed in, and I closed them behind us. Two of my men had come laden with great candles and torches, and these I had lighted and placed in golden sconces which stood out from the walls in the great hall into which we had passed through the bronze doors. When this had been done, I beckoned to Tupac, and went silently with him to the other end of the hall, where, on a throne of gold under a canopy of silver, sat a silent figure clad in the imperial robes, and with a mask of beaten gold over its face, according to the ancient custom. It was the effigy of the great Yupanqui, father of Huayna-Capac, which had been seated here since his death, as an emblem of the unbroken sovereignty of his race, giving place in turn to his son and grandson on the days that they were crowned, and being replaced when the ceremony was over.

Now, with Tupac's help I carried the effigy into a little chamber behind the throne, and there quickly removed my upper clothing and dressed myself as I had done before in the Hall of Gold, and took my place on the throne. Then I bade Tupac lead Joyful Star, with her eyes still bandaged, to me.   When he had placed her before me, I made a sign to him, and the bandage fell from her eyes.   She turned white as death, and staggered back a pace, with her hands clasped to her temples, and there she stood, staring wide-eyed at me and all the splendours about her.

Wherever her gaze wandered it saw nothing but gold and silver and gems and rich-dyed hangings of silk and wool, whose brilliant hues no time could dim.   The roof and the upper halves of the walls were covered with plates of burnished silver.   Around the walls, half-way between the floor and the ceiling, ran a great cornice or ledge of gold, on which stood the golden chairs in which were seated the mummies of the twenty Incas which I had last seen in the Sanctuary of the Sun, looking down through the eye-holes in their golden masks.

L

From the cornice to the floor hung the bright-hued hangings, and against these were ranged along the floor on either side threescore seats of silver, and the floor was paved with diamond-shaped blocks of gold and silver set alternately. Behind the throne on which I sat rose from the floor to roof a sloping wall of golden ingots, and on either hand stood a great golden vase, heaped high with unset gems, emeralds and diamonds, pearls and sapphires and rubies, precious almost beyond price; and on the roof above my throne a great, golden image of the Sun, encircled by spreading rays of gems, glowed and sparkled in the light of the candles and torches.

At last Ruth's wandering gaze became steady and rested upon my face, and I looked back into her eyes, making no sign until she should speak, and sitting motionless as the effigy whose place I had taken.

'Where am I?' she said at last in a low, faint voice, like one awakening from a dream. 'And who are you? Surely you cannot be—and yet, yes, you are Vilcaroya! What has happened?'

'Nothing more than the granting of Joyful Star's request, save that through the treasure-house which she asked to see I have brought her to a better one. Does it please her?'

'Is it real, Vilcaroya?' she whispered. 'Is all

this really gold and silver, and are these real diamonds and rubies and emeralds, or am I only dreaming? Does it please me? What a question! I have never even dreamed of anything like it. Where are we, Vilcaroya?'

'In the throne-room of the Incas, beneath what was once their palace and fortress on the hill of Sacsahuaman,' I answered, 'and this is the throne of the great Yupanqui, the greatest earthly king and conqueror of my race. I sat here and crowned myself Inca in the presence of Anda-Huillac and the priests and nobles of the Land of the Four Regions on the day before the night when I drank the death-draught with Golden Star.'

'Ah, yes, where is she?' she cried, looking round only to see that all the rest had vanished, and that she and I were alone in the great hall. 'What have they done with her, and where are Laurens and the others?' she cried, looking fearfully and almost mistrustingly at me. 'What have you done with them, Vilcaroya?'

'They are safe,' I said. 'Tupac and his men have care of them, and they will come back when I bid him bring them. But I have need of your presence here alone before I do that,' I went on, rising from my seat as I spoke. 'Has Joyful Star ever sat on a throne?'

'No,' she stammered, staring at me with

wonder in her eyes. 'You know I haven't. Why should you ask?'

'Then sit on mine,' I said, 'for I have something to say to you which I can best say and you can best hear if we change places. Nay, I will take no denial,' I said, drawing her by the hand up the steps in front of the throne, 'for it is not only your—your friend who is asking, but a crowned king in his own palace, who is lord of life and death over all who enter it.'

Half frightened and half wondering, she submitted to my will and allowed me to seat her in the chair which no woman had ever sat in before. Then I took her hand, and, dropping on one knee on the upper step, I said,—

'Joyful Star has taken one queen from me, and she alone can give me another to fill her place. She is sitting where the great Yupanqui sat when he ruled all the land from north to south, and from the eastern mountains to the sea, and ere long I too shall reign, sole and undisputed lord, over a realm wider even than that. Many things have been done that Joyful Star knows not of since I came back to my country and my people. Through all the Land of the Four Regions the word has gone forth, with the swiftness of thought, that the Son of the Sun has returned, and that the heir of the divine

Manco has come to deliver his children from bondage.*

'Everywhere the tidings have been received with joy, and the people are longing to return to the allegiance of their fathers, and tread their oppressors under foot. Before many days civil war will be raging throughout the lands of the south, and I have but to set flowing that golden stream, one of whose many sources is here, and say, "Here is gold and silver in plenty for all who will fight under the Rainbow Banner," and I shall have armies and fleets to do what I will with, and the sway of my sceptre shall reach from north to south and sea to sea.

'This I shall do because of my oath; but I have brought Joyful Star here to tell her, in the most sacred place that is left in the Land of the Four Regions, that I shall also do it so that she, if she will, may be queen where I am king, and sit beside me on my throne, and make my empire a paradise by the brightness and the sweetness of her presence. I cannot forget, as she bade me do —for the words that I said in the heat of my

* The Inca Indians of the Sierra region possess the same extra-ordinary faculty of transmitting intelligence without apparent material means that the Hindoos and the Arabs have. Thus, during the last revolution in Peru, the fall of Lima was known to the Indians of Bolivia on the southern shore of Lake Titicaca three days after it happened, though the telegraph wires were cut and all ordinary communications suspended. Without the telegraph this would be quite impossible by any means known to Europeans.

passion are true—for I love you, Joyful Star, and all that I have or shall ever have on earth will be worthless to me unless you take it as a gift from my hands. Nay, do not speak, for now I seek no answer, whether good or evil. I have brought you here that I, as a king, might kneel at the feet of her whom I would win for my queen, and from now until I sit in the sight of all the world on the throne of the Four Regions no other words of love shall pass my lips. So you shall have many days to ponder what I have said, and to ask your own heart whether it will say "yes" or "no" to me when I stretch out my hand from my throne and ask you to come and sit beside me and rule my people with me.'

Before she could answer, I stood up and clapped my hands, and Tupac with six others, dressed now in the forbidden costume of their ancestors, entered the hall from the ante-chamber, into which they had taken the others, and came towards me, bearing wands across their shoulders in token of homage, and with heads downbent, not daring to look upon my majesty till I bade them. I drew Joyful Star from the throne by the hand, and seating myself in it, said in the ancient tongue,—

'Let the Children of the Blood enter into the presence of their father and their lord, and let the strangers be brought in, and the other maiden, all with eyes bandaged, and let seats of silver be placed to the right and left of the throne, one for each of the virgins of the Sun to sit upon. Are all things else ready, Tupac-Rayca?'

'Yes, lord,' he answered, stepping out in front of the others and falling on his knees, 'and the Children of the Blood are waiting to see the glory of thy presence and hear the words of wisdom and hope from thy lips.'

CHAPTER VIII

HOW THE SOUL OF GOLDEN STAR CAME BACK

WHEN the two chairs had been brought in and placed according to my orders, I rose from my throne and led Joyful Star to the one on my left hand and placed her in it, still silent with the wonder and perplexity of what she had seen and heard since her eyes were opened. Then, seating myself again, I bade Tupac summon the Children of the Blood to take their places, and presently he ushered them in from the chambers that opened out of the great hall on either hand at the other end.

There were threescore of them, the heads of the families of Ayllos, whose blood was the purest and whose descent was most direct from the old nobility of my own days. Each of them, too, under the outward husk of his forlorn and degraded state, had preserved unsullied the ancient faith and traditions of the sacred race, and,

against all appearances, had steadfastly hoped
for the fulfilment of the promises that had been
given in the olden times. More than this, too—
each had treasured, as a miser hoards his gold,
the ever-growing legacy of hate which the oppression and contempt of the Spaniards and their
meaner descendants had heaped up from generation to generation against the long-awaited day
of vengeance which, as but two or three in
that strange company alone knew, was now so
near at hand.

Ever since I had revealed myself to them in the
Hall of Gold they had been working for the end in
view with the swift, subtle arts known only to those
of their race, and already, from Quito in the north
to Santiago in the south, tidings had gone forth
that the day of deliverance was approaching, and
that ere long the Rainbow Banner would be raised
by the hands of him for whom the Children of the
Sun had waited.

Each of the fathers of the people was dressed,
as Tupac was, in the long-forbidden garb of the
ancient nobility, and each as he entered stopped in
the centre of the hall and paid his homage before
he went to his seat. Then, when all were seated,
I ordered that the strangers should be brought in,
and they were led into the midst of the silent
assembly, with their eyes still bandaged. Over
Golden Star's head a veil had been thrown, hiding

her face, for it was my purpose that it should not be seen for the present, and how strangely this purpose worked you shall soon see.

As she came up the middle of the hall, following Tupac, who was leading her as obedient as a little child, I descended from the throne and went to meet her, and led her to the seat on my right hand and placed her in it. Francis Hartness, the professor and Djama I left standing in the middle of the hall, each with one of Tupac's chosen guards beside him. When Golden Star was seated, I stood up in front of the throne and said to those assembled, speaking in the ancient tongue,—

'Sons of the Blood and fathers of the Oppressed, you know already how the promise that was made by our Father the Sun, through the lips of his high priest, in the days when first the oppressors came, has been in part most faithfully and marvellously fulfilled. I, Vilcaroya —son of Huayna-Capac, son of the great Yupanqui Inca, before whose throne-seat I am now standing alive in your presence—am he of whom it was said that one who should pass from life to life through the shadows of death should grasp the sceptre of the divine Manco, and restore the ancient glory of the Children of the Sun. And with me, as you know, there was another, at whose call and for love of whom

I dared the ordeal of the death-sleep and swore the oath which I have returned to the world of living men to fulfil. I have already given you some proof that I am what I say I am, for I have revealed to you secrets which were buried in the grave with me and in those faithful hearts which have been pulseless now for many generations.

'But now, that all things may be made plain to you, and that no doubts may remain in your hearts to hinder the working of our sacred purpose, I have brought here before you witnesses of the wonders that have been worked —even those who wrought them themselves, that their own lips may tell you the story; and with them I have brought yet another witness who, though she cannot speak to you in our ancient tongue, of which our Father, for his own wise purposes, has deprived her during her long sleep, will yet in her own person and even with silent lips be witness enough that I have not lied to you. Now let the eyes of the strangers be uncovered and their mouths opened that they may see and speak.'

Even as the words left my lips they were obeyed, and at the same time I stretched out my right hand and raised the veil from the head of Golden Star, and unloosed the bandage from her eyes.

A deep murmur of wonder ran round the hall; a sharp cry of amazement broke from Djama's lips, and the two others stared blankly about them. Then I raised my left hand to command silence, and, still speaking the ancient speech and pointing with my right hand to Golden Star, said,—

'This, O Fathers of the People, is she who drank the death-draught with me. This is Cory-Coyllur, daughter of Huayna - Capac, and sister of the long-ago murdered Huascar, and my sister, too, since her great father was mine also. With her, as the tradition was told to you, I plighted the marriage - troth before the altar in the Sanctuary of the Sun, and of that troth I would speak to you now. Such marriage is no longer lawful in the world to which we have returned, and in token of this our Father the Sun has sent this other likeness of Golden Star, who sits upon my left hand, to tell me that it may not be; and to make the message surer, it has pleased him also to put into my heart a love for her differing from, though not greater than that which I have borne for Golden Star, and if my Father who has given me this love shall also look with kindness upon my longing, then Joyful Star, as I have named her, shall be my Coya* and my queen, and Golden Star shall

* The queen-consort of the Inca, as distinguished from the many others whom the ancient laws allowed him to marry.

be her sister and mine, and I doubt not that in his own good time our Father will send her a fitting mate, that her heart may not be empty nor her life lonely.'

As I said these last words I saw the eyes of all who were sitting in the chairs turn, as if moved by one impulse, and rest on Francis Hartness, standing strong and stately in the midst of the little group in the middle of the hall, overtopping the others by nearly a span, and crowned with his curling golden hair; and as I, too, looked at him, a new thought came into my mind, and I spoke aloud again and said,—

'Yes, Brothers of the Blood, I read your thought. The stranger from the land which is the greatest of all lands in the world of to-day, is a true Son of the Sun, though not of our blood, for his heart is clean and his tongue is straight and his arm strong, and perchance it may please our Father to bring about that which he has put into our hearts.'

At this another murmur ran round the hall, and every head was bowed in assent.

Now all this time the three Englishmen had been standing patiently in the midst of the hall, looking about them at its splendours, and waiting till I should speak to them, for the professor knew enough of the Quichua tongue to follow what I had been saying, and had told the others that I was speaking of them. Now I spoke to them in English, and told them what I had brought them to the throne-room for, and then I had chairs placed for them at top of the hall, to my left hand.

When they had taken their places, I asked the professor to speak in Spanish to those assembled, and tell them whether or not the story of my return to life was true, and whether or not Golden Star had been found where Anda-Huillac and the priests had placed her, and had been, like me, restored to life by the arts of Djama his friend. This he did in few, straight words, and after him Djama rose at my bidding and told them also what he had done. When he had finished I took the Llautu from my head and raised it above me with outstretched arms and said in a loud voice,—

' If you, O Children of the Blood and Sons of the Ancient Race, believe now that I am in truth Vilcaroya, son of Huayna-Capac, and lawful heir of the divine Manco, from whom all the Incas of our race draw their royal blood, then take me for your lord as my father was the lord of your fathers; or if any shall have yet doubt in his heart, let him speak now or for ever be silent.'

Then with one accord they rose from their seats and came before me and prostrated themselves on the shining pavement of the throne-room, and began to chant, in a low, soft tone, the Song of Homage with which of old the new-crowned Incas had been hailed, generation after generation, Sons of the Sun and lords of life and death throughout the Land of the Four Regions.

And now a wondrous thing happened. As I stood there facing the prostrate throng, lowering the Llautu on to my head, I heard a low, sharp cry beside me on my right hand. I turned half round, and there I saw Golden Star staring at me with eyes burning with the light that shone through them from her new-awakened soul.

Her hands were clasped to her temples, pushing back her thick, bright hair from her forehead. Her face was flushed, and her half-open lips were working as though they were striving to shape some long-forgotten words. At the instant that the Llautu touched my brows, she rose to her feet. Then a cry burst from her lips and went ringing down the hall, and the next moment she had thrown herself forward and I had caught her in my arms.

As I did so our eyes met, and our hearts looked at each other through them. In that one burning glance the mists of the long years were melted, all things else were forgotten, and for the moment we stood alone—the children of a long-dead generation — in the solitude that our strange fate had made about us. Then her lips moved, not dumbly this time, and in a voice that woke, who shall say how many memories in my heart, she said,—

'Have they awakened us, my lord? Tell me how long we have slept, my Vilcaroya. It seems long to me, and I have had strange, dim dreams, and thought I was not one, but two, and that one of myselves was your sister and the other was your Coya and queen. It was strange, was it not, to dream like that?'

'Not so strange but that it may be true, O my sister, Golden Star,' I said, my wonder for the moment overcome by a new hope that uprose within me at her words. 'Stranger things than that have happened since we fell asleep together in the distant days that are no more. See, Ñusta mi, here is your other self, the living shape of that sister-soul of yours, who has watched over you and cared for you and loved you since you drew the first breath of your new life. She cannot speak our tongue, for she is the daughter of another age than ours, but she has taught me hers and I will speak for you.'

As I said this I took her hands from where they rested on my shoulders, and led her to the seat of Joyful Star, who was standing in front of it, with one hand on the arm of her chair and the other one clasped to her heart, her face white with fear and her eyes wide with wonder.

'What has happened, Vilcaroya?' she said, in a voice so low that it was almost a whisper. 'Has her memory come back, and does she believe herself to be your — your wife?'

As she forced the last word from her hesitating lips I saw the hot blood flow into her cheeks, and a new light that shot like a dart of fire into my heart leapt into her eyes.

'No,' I said, with a smile that was quickly answered by one that came unawares to her lips. 'She calls herself my sister and me her lord, and says that she has dreamed that she is not one but two, and that her other sister - self is Vilcaroya's wife and queen. Now, if that dream may be the truth, tell her so!'

And with that I took her hand gently from

where it rested on the chair and laid Golden Star's in it.

'But—I cannot speak your language, and she wouldn't understand me,' she said softly, with one swift glance at me and another longer look at Golden Star's smiling face, so wondrous like her own.

'There is another speech than that of the tongue,' I answered, 'which all men understand.'

'Yes!' she said, and then she drew Golden Star gently to her and kissed her.

All this while the Ayllos had remained silent and prostrate before the throne, none daring to raise their heads till I bade them, and the three Englishmen sat still, hearing what I had said to Joyful Star and her answer to it, and yet neither speaking nor rising from their seats, each full of his own thoughts and not willing to betray his feelings by any rash word that he might speak in the wonder of the moment. But now I turned with my heart full of joy and new hope, and said in a voice in which my gladness seemed to sing like a bird in the morning sky,—

'Rise up, Brothers of the Blood, and look upon your lord and rejoice with him, for our Father the Sun has looked kindly upon him and filled all his life with light. He has given back memory and speech to Golden Star, his daughter, and put it into the heart of Joyful Star, her other sister-self, to love her and to make plain that which might else have been dark.'

Then they all rose to their feet and saluted me and paid their homage to Golden Star and Joyful Star as well, and then I waved them to their seats, and when they had gone I led Golden Star back to her chair, and then I called Djama to me, and when he came and stood before me I said,—

'You have seen what has happened, and you have heard the words that have been said. You see now that there is no need for Golden Star to go to England. Therefore it remains but for you and for your friend to take the treasure that is yours, and for us to say farewell.'

'And Ruth?' he asked. 'You know, of course, that that will mean farewell to her also.'

I could see that he was ill at ease, and that his words were not the words that his true thoughts would have spoken. As I looked at him I saw that his eyes shifted and wandered from my gaze, and I said coldly,—

'Much has happened since we last spoke of this. It will be for Joyful Star herself to say whether she will bid me farewell or not. Is she not free to go or stay where she pleases? Say, now, when I shall command the treasure to be taken out of the Hall of Gold for you, and where you wish it to be placed.'

'I must ask you to give me time to think about that and talk it over with the professor,' he said, 'for we have no means of taking such an immense amount of gold to the coast and getting it on board ship without suspicion.'

'Go, then,' I said, 'and speak with him, but remember that it must be done quickly, for ere many days are past there will be war in the land, and neither your lives nor your gold will be safe.'

'I will take good care of that,' he said in a tone whose strangeness told me more than his words, and with that he turned away and sat down beside the professor, with the thoughts that were within his heart still unspoken. As soon as he had gone back to his seat I called Francis Hartness to me and set him beside me on the right hand of the throne, and then I told who he was and showed that he was well skilled in those new arts of warfare which had taken the place of our ancient methods, and how he had promised to use his knowledge for me and lead my armies into battle, hazarding his own life on the chance of our success; and when I had said this I named him leader of all those who should range themselves under the Rainbow Banner when the day of battle came, and bade all present obey his orders and enforce obedience to them, even as though his commands were my own.

Then I bade Francis Hartness himself speak all that was in his mind freely and without fear of betrayal concerning the war that was soon to be waged between the rival factions of our oppressors and the means that were to be used to turn their strife to our own account, and this he did, speaking in fluent Spanish and in short, clear sentences, as a man of action and a soldier should speak.

He told how he had made himself acquainted with the forces on both sides, and how, with the help of Tupac, he had sounded the feelings of those by whom the fighting would have to be done, and had found them willing to leave the service of the schemers who sought to make themselves tyrants over the land, and fight for those whose purpose it was to restore the ancient rule and give liberty to all to use their lives as they thought best and to win for themselves as many of the gifts of the All-Father as they were able to do. He told, too, how he had sent many messages over the lightning-wires to his own country, bidding friends like himself in war to come out as quickly as might be to find the fortune that awaited them, yet saying nothing of war but only of gold that was to be had for the taking.

When he had finished, I bade Tupac summon all who were present to the foot of the throne, and then I spoke to them of the plans that I had made with Francis Hartness in all their details, and showed them how each, according to his opportunities, could give his help in carrying them out, and then, as by this time the night was far spent and there was yet work of another sort to do, I sent them back to their seats, and calling Ruth and Golden Star to me, I bade them follow me, and led the way down the hall and through one of the passages at the end until I brought them to a chamber which Tupac and his comrades had already prepared for them by my orders, and here I left them to take their rest together, promising to return in the morning.

When I got back into the throne-room Djama asked me whither I had taken his sister, and I told him what I had done, saying that the hour was now too late for us to return to our home on the other side of the valley, and that, moreover, it was needful for us to go back to the Hall of Gold to make a proper count of the treasure and to let him and the professor swear their oaths of secrecy in the presence of the fathers of my people.

Then I left him, looking much more ill at ease than such tidings should have made him feel, and told Tupac in the ancient tongue to take three of his companions and go and do that which it was now time to do. So he went and chose his men and departed through the bronze doors by which we had entered the hall. After that I named a guard to remain all night in the hall, and bade the rest go and put on their everyday clothing, and I, too, went back into the chamber behind the throne and changed my imperial garments for the others that I had put off.

Then I ordered the torches and candles to be extinguished, all saving a few that were left for the guards, and then the eyes of Djama and the professor were bandaged afresh, though those of Francis Hartness—he being now one of us and devoted to our cause—were left open ; and when this was done the lanterns were lit and I led the way into the ante-chamber of the throne-room, where the bronze doors still stood open as Tupac had left them.

I stood by them till the last man had passed out, then I went through and closed them. Then I followed the rest and again placed myself at their head. But when we reached the end of the straight passage, instead of turning the revolving pillar which closed the entrance of the winding passage leading to the Hall of Gold, I sought about with my lantern on the floor until I found three marks in the shape of a triangle in one corner of a great square slab of stone, and, taking a long staff which one of the men carried, I placed the end on the triangle and calling two others to help me, we bore downwards with all, our weight, and when we had thrust awhile on the staff the corner of the slab sank into the floor and it turned on a diagonal axis until it stood upright, leaving a three-cornered space large enough for a man's body to pass through easily. Then I made a sign to one of the Ayllos and said,—

'Anahuac, take your lantern down there and light the way down the steps.'

'Truly there are no secrets in the land hidden from the eyes of our Lord!' he said, glancing round in wonder at the rest, and then he lowered himself with his lantern into the hole and disappeared.

Then I bade the rest follow him one by one, and so all went down, I going last with Francis Hartness, who helped me to put the stone back into its place.

Our way now led along a rough-hewn gallery that sloped gently upwards for some twelve hundred paces, and at the end of it there was a little chamber measuring some twenty feet each way and having no apparent outlet, but in the middle of one of the walls there was another of the cunningly-constructed revolving stones which our ancient masons ever used to bar their secret ways, and this three of our men, working as I told them, turned on its hinge, and through the opening that was thus made we passed out in single file to a little rock-walled valley over which the stars were shining.

The door was closed behind us, and dust and dirt were rubbed over the thin lines which marked where it fitted into the rock, and then we extinguished our lanterns and passed out of the valley on to the pampa.

The place where we had come out was about a thousand paces from the walls of the Sacsa-huaman. We halted on the plain and I gave my last orders to the Ayllos. Then we set out in the direction of the Fortress, and as we went one by one my followers disappeared silently into the half darkness about us till at last only four of them were left, two leading Djama and two the professor.

I had been talking of many things with Francis Hartness on the way, and showing him how in the olden times we had made use of the secret passages such as those he had already seen, and when we saw that we had come out by a way different to that which we had entered, he asked me the reason of it, and I answered him in a low voice and said,—

'Because the other way is closed. Have patience a little while and you shall see why.'

Then we went on our way in silence until we came to the edge of the valley in which the Sayacusca stands. Here I halted and whispered a few words to the men who were leading Djama and the professor. They slipped off their ponchos and threw them over the heads of their prisoners, for such the two were now to be for the present. I heard a muffled cry from Djama, and I went to him and put my hand on his shoulder and said in a whisper,—

'Keep quiet and lie down. These men have knives and will use them at my bidding.'

Then they pulled him and the professor down, and they lay quiet, knowing that their lives were in my hands, and I lay down on the edge of the valley, signing to Francis Hartness to come and lie beside me. Then I pointed into the valley and bade him watch. Presently, in the dim light, we made out figures moving about the rock, and caught every now and then the glint of the star-rays along thin lines of polished metal.

'Rifle barrels!' he whispered. 'What are they doing here? I didn't know that your men had any weapons yet.'

'No,' I said, 'those are in the hands of soldiers from Cuzco. The time has come sooner than I thought for, and yet not too soon. You will see the first blow struck for the freedom of my people before to-morrow's sun rises.'

CHAPTER IX

THE TREACHERY OF DJAMA

'WAIT now for a little while with patience,' I said, laying my hand on his shoulder, 'and you shall see a strange thing, a thing that shall show you how strong the old traditions are still in the land of the Incas. Lie here and do not let yourself be seen till I send a messenger for you. It will not be very long.'

He nodded and I rose quietly to my feet and went round the hollow until I got the great stone between me and the place where the soldiers were standing, and then I went down on my hands and knees and crept quietly towards it and climbed up a flight of steps carved in it. This took me to the top of the cleft in which is the broken stairway. I climbed down this and dropped softly into the hole at the bottom. It was dry now, for Tupac had done that which I had bidden him in the throne-room. I felt my way down the steps till I came to the wall at the bottom. Then I whispered his name, and he answered out of the darkness in the old language,—

'I am here, Lord, and all that has been ordered is done.'

I crept towards him along the wall, measuring my way along it with my outstretched arms till I knew that I had come to the revolving stone which closed the way into the hall. He was standing against it, and one of the others was with him. I felt over the door till I found the silver socket, and then we opened the door as before with the bar which Tupac had brought. Then I went down through the hall and lighted a lantern and went into the little chamber where, as before, I changed my clothing for the imperial robes, and set the Llautu on my head; but I kept on my belt under my cloak, and put two revolvers in it in case I should need them, and when I went back into the hall Tupac and the others were lighting candles and putting them in the holders round the walls as I had bidden them. When this was done I said to him,—

'Go now and bring the others down, first the soldiers with their officer, by whose side you must keep closely, and see that your knife is ready. Then let Ainu bring the Men of the Blood, and the strangers quickly after them, and bid Anahauc and Ainu close the door when the last man has entered.'

He bowed his head, and the two went out and left me sitting there on a seat built up of blocks of gold before the pyramid, waiting to play my part in the scene that was to follow, and strike the first blow in the battle that I had come to fight. Presently I heard the rattle of arms and the sound of footsteps coming along the passage. I took one of the revolvers out of my belt and held it ready under my cloak, and sat still and rigid as the effigy of Yupanqui, looking straight before me at the entrance at the other end.

Tupac came in first, and close behind him was a Spanish officer with a drawn sword in his hand. After him came the soldiers, two and two, with their rifles and bayonets. The officer stopped and stared about him, blinking with eyes half dazzled by the sudden light and the glitter of the gold and jewels which he saw wherever he looked. The same instant I saw the gleam of steel in Tupac's hand close to his yellow throat. Then he said to him in Spanish,—

'Put up your sword, señor, and come with

me and beg your life from the Son of the Sun who sits yonder on his throne.'

The Spaniard uttered a loud cry of amazement as his eyes fell upon me, for so far he had not seen me, having been too much taken up by the splendours of the hall. Then he turned and called to his soldiers, but while the cry was still in his throat, Tupac's arm went round his neck and the knife-point touched his skin. Then he bade two of the soldiers take the sword out of his hand and hold him fast, which they did, greatly to his wonder, for he did not know that the betrayer was already betrayed. As soon as he was safe, Tupac told the other soldiers to take their places along the walls, and they did so in silence, yet wondering greatly at all they saw. There were four-and-twenty of them, not counting the two who held the officer, all men of Indian blood whom the Spaniards * had made rather slaves than soldiers to fight their petty quarrels for them for little pay and scanty food.

After them came Anahuac and Ainu and the rest of the Men of the Blood, bringing with them Djama and the professor blindfolded, and Francis Hartness with his eyes unbound. All this time I had neither moved nor made a

* The Inca naturally does not distinguish between the modern Peruvians and their Spanish ancestors.

sound, and the soldiers were looking at me almost in terror, wondering whether I was truly a man or one of the dead Incas with living eyes in his head. As for the Spanish officer, being a coward, as many of his sort are, he was already white with fear, and his knees were shaking as he stood between the two soldiers who held him. When all had entered, Anahauc came and prostrated himself before me and said,—

'The commands of the Son of the Sun are obeyed. All are here, and the door is shut.'

Before I answered him, I called Francis Hartness to me and said,—

'Come here and stand by me, my friend, for I shall need your counsel.'

He came and stood by me on my right hand, saying as he looked still wonderingly at me,—

'This means treachery, I suppose, and after that, tragedy. Is that why you left Ruth and Golden Star in the Fortress? I am afraid you had only too much reason to, but I hope, for Ruth's sake, you will do justice with as much mercy as you can.'

'You shall see,' I answered. 'But if it were not for her you would see justice without mercy.'

Then I bade Anahuac rise, and told him

and Tupac to unbind the eyes of Djama and the professor and bring them before me.

As Djama's eyes opened to the light, he stared about him in silence for a moment. His face was very pale, and his lips were twitching and trembling. The professor, too, looked about him, also wondering greatly at what he saw; but neither of them spoke till they had been led forward and stood before me. Then, while Djama still kept silence, the professor, looking from me to Hartness, said in a voice that had much wonder, but no fear or sign of guilt, in it,—

'What is this? What does all this mean? What are all these soldiers here for, Vilcaroya? I thought it was so important that all this should be kept secret? Surely no one has betrayed you already? But no, that can't be. Hartness, what does it all mean?'

'It means—first,' I said, speaking very slowly, and not in a loud voice, 'that you have been brought here with Laurens Djama to take the oath which you agreed to take—never to reveal the secrets of the things that you have learned. I ask your pardon for the rude way in which my people have brought you, but it was necessary.'

Then I turned to Djama, who was standing silent and motionless, with clenched teeth and set face, like one who knows that he stands near his doom and has no hope of mercy, and said,—

'Now, Laurens Djama, are you ready to do as you promised to do when I told you that I would give you the half of this gold for what you have done for me and Golden Star? Are you ready to swear the oath here, in the presence of these witnesses, that you swore to me then?'

He drew himself up and looked at me boldly —for he was a brave man although his heart was black—and said to me with a hard, harsh laugh in his voice,—

'You have been too clever for me, and so I suppose you have the right to mock me. There is no need to go on with this farce. The sight of your treasures gave me the gold-fever, I suppose, and it drove me mad, as it has driven many others mad, and I betrayed you. There is no use saying any more. I see that I have been betrayed too, and that my life is in your hands, so I need only say that I keep the right of taking it myself in my own way.'

'There is no need for that yet,' I said, 'and others are concerned in this besides you.'

Then I turned from him to Francis Hartness and said,—

'I cannot speak the Spanish speech, and I would not if I could. Do you therefore speak to the Spaniard yonder, and bid him say how he came to be here with his soldiers. Tell him, too, that if he lies, or refuses to speak, he shall be buried in the gold he came to steal until the weight of it crushes his life out. But say to him that if he speaks the truth and holds nothing back and does as I shall bid him, he shall have his life, and afterwards as much gold as three men can carry.'

So then Francis Hartness turned to the trembling Spaniard and questioned him, and he confessed freely as soon as he knew he was not to be killed, and told how Djama had gone to the Governor of Cuzco and told him of my coming and of a great treasure that he would show him, and of others that I knew the secret of and might be made to reveal, and how he had bargained that half of all that was found should be his and the other half the Governor's, if he would help him to carry it to the coast in safety and put it on a steamer. The Spaniard told also how the Governor, who was his own father, had only half believed this story, and had bidden him bring a company of soldiers to the appointed place and see if there was any truth in Djama's story, and, if he found there was, to take Djama and all of us prisoners and carry us back to Cuzco, and put us into the prison until he could question us the next day.

When he had finished, Djama laughed again and said,—

'There's the honour of a Peruvian! Serve me right for being such a fool as to trust to it!'

But I bade him sternly to hold his peace till he should be told to speak, and then, when Francis Hartness had told me in English what the Spaniard had said, I bade Tupac and Anahuac stand forward and tell of their share in what had been done, so that all might understand. They told their story in Quichua, and when I translated it into English to Francis Hartness I made few words of it, of which the meaning was this,—

Ever since Tupac and his comrades had recognised me as their lord, and sworn their faith to me, they, and others whom they trusted, had industriously spread abroad the news of my coming — though telling nothing that would make a traitor able to betray us— and, in proof of their story, little wedges of gold, stamped with the ancient symbol of the Sun, had been passed from hand to hand as earnest of my promise that I would use the hidden treasures of the Incas for the benefit of my people, and make money of gold where now there was only silver and copper.

By this time, not only had the golden wedges gone far and wide through the land, but nearly all the soldiers of the pure Indian blood had been won over to my cause, for, as I have said, and as everyone in the country knows, these soldiers are treated with great hardness by their Spanish masters, who often pay them nothing for many weeks or months together, and give them scanty food and hard usage, and cast them into prison or flog them and shoot them if they think to do anything to get justice. Moreover, there are always factions of men they call politicians scheming for power and setting the soldiers fighting against one another and against their countrymen for no benefit to themselves. So what Francis Hartness had told me on the night that Golden Star had come back to life had already begun to come true. More than half the garrison of Cuzco had already been won over, and only waited for the signal which should bid the whole Indian population of the valley to rise and seize the arms and ammunition in the city, and make the officers and the Governor and all the officials prisoners.

Anahuac's daughter was a servant in the

Governor's house, and this girl understood Spanish, though she pretended only to know Quichua and the dialect of the people, and she had been set to watch,* and Tupac's eldest son had also been secretly watching all the comings and goings of Djama since we came to Cuzco. In this way his visit to the Governor had been made known to me, and then one of the soldiers in the company that had been ordered to go with the Governor's son to the Rodadero had told Tupac of the order, and I had arranged with him how the surprise was to be carried out, and this, as you have seen, had been done with complete success.

When I had finished telling this to Hartness I turned to the professor and said to him kindly,—

'There has been nothing said that brings any share of the guilt of this treason to you, so now, if you will promise me on your faith and honour as an Englishman to keep my secrets and obey such commands as I shall put upon you for your own safety and that of all of us, you shall go free, and you shall have the choice of going back to England or to any other country until the war is over, or of staying here under my protection until

---

* This is quite a common thing in Peru, and the Indian women make exceedingly clever spies.

you can go away safely with the treasure which shall be yours. But if you go now you cannot take it with you, for in a few days from now there will be war throughout the whole land, and it would be impossible to take so much treasure to the coast. Now, what do you say?'

He thought for a moment and then said,—

'I am not a man of war, as you know Vilcaroya, but I hope I am a man of honour. I have never breathed a syllable that could have given anyone an inkling of your secret, and I promise you solemnly that I never will. What Djama has done distresses me even more than it amazes me. I would have staked my life on his honesty, and if you will release him and let him come with me—'

'No, no, my friend!' I said, quickly and sternly. 'What you would ask is impossible. His aims were deeper and his sin was blacker than it has been shown to be here. He did not betray us for gold alone, for he knew that I would keep my promise and give him more than he could want. He would have given me to my enemies to be killed—it might have been by tortures, to make me say where my treasures were hidden—so that he might have had Golden Star at his mercy.'

'It was your own fault, curse you! Why

did you not give her to me?' Djama cried suddenly, breaking loose from the two who held his arms and putting his hand to his pistol pocket. The next instant my own revolver was out from under my cloak and levelled at his heart.

'Another motion and I will kill you,' I said, 'though so quick a death would be too good for you. Tie his hands behind his back and hold him faster this time. Give me his pistol.'

Before I had done speaking they had seized him again in spite of his struggles, and paying no heed to his cries and imprecations—for by this time his long-pent-up passion had broken loose and made him almost mad, and when they had given me his pistol I said to him,—

'I told you that Golden Star should be yours if you could win her as an honest man. But you sought to steal her as you would have stolen my gold. That is enough; keep silence now, or you shall be gagged.'

Then I held out my hand to the professor and said,—

'I will accept your promise, for you are an honest man. There is my hand. Now we will be friends as before, and I will answer for your safety. Will you go or stay with us?'

'I will stay,' he said, 'for my studies are not completed yet, and besides, I am anxious to see what the Inca empire will be like when it is restored.'

'I am glad that you say so,' I replied, 'for you are welcome, and you shall make your home here always if you will.'

Then I bade them stand the Spanish officer in the professor's place beside Djama, and, turning to Francis Hartness, said,—

'These men are worthy of death, for they would have delivered us to death, but I cannot kill Djama since Joyful Star might hate me for it, and if I do not kill him it would not be justice to kill the Spaniard. What shall I do?'

'I see nothing for it,' he said, after thinking awhile, 'but shutting them up safely until we have got this business over, and then sending them out of the country and forbidding them to come back under pain of death. There are plenty of places that they would be perfectly safe in.'

'That is well thought of, my friend,' I said, and it shall be done. They came for gold and they shall have it. They shall live in it, and see gold, and nothing but gold, till the sight of it is hateful to them. They shall have a prison of gold, and eat and drink from gold, and sleep and walk and sit on gold. Yes, truly, they shall have enough of gold before they see the light of day again. Now tell the Spaniard what I have said.'

He did so, and at first the wretch's eyes glittered and then grew dim when the true meaning of his doom came upon him, for it meant he knew not how long an imprisonment with a man who had betrayed his friends, and whom, as he had confessed, he would himself have betrayed ; and he thought, too, that I had only promised him his life and the gold to make him speak, and that now I would keep him prisoner and perhaps kill him in the end. So he fell on his knees, like the craven that he was, and begged for mercy, and told Hartness of my promise, and with Hartness's lips I told him only that he must have patience and wait until it was my pleasure to do what I had said.

After this I called Tupac and Anahuac and told them what I wished done, and they took a score of their men and forthwith began to build, in a corner of the hall beside the throne, a chamber measuring some ten feet each way, of the oblong blocks of gold which were piled up in the pyramid, and while they were doing this I called the soldiers before me and told them, speaking in their own dialect, that if they were faithful to me until the end of the war, each man should have one ounce weight of gold paid to him every month, and one ounce more for each of his comrades that he could persuade to join us, and for this night's work I would give them each a wedge of gold of the weight of two ounces, which was more money than all that they had earned in their lives before; and when I had promised this they went on their knees and swore faith to me and destruction to their hated Spanish masters.

Then I told them how Francis Hartness would lead them to battle and to victory as he had led the soldiers of his own nation, and after that he spoke to them in Spanish, and told them what to tell their comrades and what was to be done with the arms and ammunition when the signal for the rising was given.

All this while Djama and the Spaniard were kept standing watching the building of their golden prison-cell. The men worked swiftly, and the many hands made the toil light, and they built the walls up very thick and strong, fitting the golden bricks closely into each other, and making the walls smooth and without hand or foot-hold, so that neither could any of the bricks be got out, nor the walls be climbed. The cell was divided into two by another wall, and when the walls were finished they were about ten feet high, and there was an opening into each cell in front, large enough for a man to crawl in on his hands and knees.

When all was ready I said to Djama,—

'There is your house of gold. Go and dwell in it 'till it shall be safe for me to release you. Every day, as I have said, you shall eat and drink from plates and cups of gold, and you shall dream of gold until this gold-fever of yours is cured.'

'Until I have gone gold-mad, you mean!' he cried, snarling at me like an angry dog. 'It is just such a vengeance as a half-civilised savage would have thought of. You know as well as I do that I shall go mad in there unless I kill myself first.'

'You have your choice!' I said. 'I will make your punishment no lighter. If you think to pull the walls down they will fall on you and crush you, and you will be buried in gold, and if I am told that you have tried to break out, I will put chains of gold on you, so heavy that you shall not be able to drag them across your cell; but if you are peaceful and patient, all your wants shall be attended to by those that I shall appoint, and you shall have everything but liberty and the light of day. Now, go in.'

'I won't!' he cried with a curse that ended in a scream. 'I shall go mad in there, I tell you, and that is a thousand times worse than death to me. I won't! Damn you, I won't!'

'Then you shall be thrust in,' I said.

They thrust him in with his arms still bound.

To face page 205.

I made a sign to those who held him, and they, seeing what I meant, took him by the body and the legs, and carried him, feet foremost, kicking and struggling, towards the hole. Then they thrust him in with his arms still bound. But when he was half-way through, I bade one of them loose the cords a little, so that he could free himself afterwards. The Spaniard made no resistance, and when he was bidden crept, trembling like a hound that has been flogged, into his cell, and when they were both in I ordered the openings to be built up.

Francis Hartness and the professor had gone away to the other end of the hall, not liking to see this, and yet knowing that it would be useless to seek to persuade me to more mercy.

'Our work here is done now,' I said, going to them, 'and it would be well for us to go back to the fortress and sleep, for the morning is near and there will be much work to do before long.'

'I don't think I shall sleep much after what I have seen to-night,' said Hartness, 'and if I did sleep I think I should dream of that golden prison and those two poor wretches hungering and thirsting for daylight and liberty, with the means of buying any luxury the world could give them within reach of their hands.'

'Yes,' said the professor, 'it is a curious situation, isn't it?—quite apart from the personal interest it has for us. Now, in England or America, a room built with walls and floor of solid gold would be a luxury that only a millionaire could afford, and he would probably be thought a fool for building it, and yet here it is only a prison in which a man might well starve to death. Come, let us get away from here. I really don't want to hear any more of Djama's ravings than I can help. Good heavens! who ever would have thought that a man of his culture and learning and strength of mind could possibly have made such a blackguard of himself!'

'Well,' said Hartness, with a dry sort of laugh, 'you see he was the victim of the two passions that have done most to drive men mad or make scoundrels of them since the world began—the love of woman and the lust for gold. I don't pretend to understand it myself, because he had gold enough promised to him, and there is no telling but that he might have won the woman; but there, you never can tell how far any man is mad or sane until he's tried.'

'But there was something else, my friend,' I said. 'There was, as you say, lust of gold and love of woman; but there was also hate. Why, I know not; but though I owe my new life to that man, I have hated him and he has hated me

since we learnt to know each other as living men.
You know, too, how, as I told you, Golden Star
shrank from him as though he had been a poison-
ous reptile, and yet why should I hate him and
yet love her who is of the same flesh and blood
as he is?'

'I would rather discuss the problem in the
open air or at the hacienda than here,' said the
professor, 'and even then I don't suppose we
should get much nearer to a solution, for these
things are mysteries and mostly past finding out.
Yet it may be that you and he, the sons of
different centuries, may actually have embodied
in you the differences and the antipathies of
the two ages and the two races to which you
belong. There is no telling. But come, let us
get out of here, please. I really can't stand this
any longer.'

'Nor I,' said Hartness. 'For goodness' sake
let us go! This is a good deal more trying to
the nerves than a cavalry charge or a smart
skirmish.'

'Very well,' I said, 'we will go.'

Then I called to Tupac and bade him tell the
soldiers and the rest that the night's work was
over and it was time to go. We gave each of the
soldiers his wedge of gold, as I had promised
them; and once more I made them swear that
each would kill any of the others who thought

to betray us. Then Tupac and Anahuac went and opened the stone door, and we returned from the Hall of Gold to the upper earth, leaving Djama and his fellow traitor still raving and crying within the walls of their golden prison.

CHAPTER X

ON THE RODADERO

FRANCIS HARTNESS and I came last out of
the passage, and I asked him to lead the
soldiers out of the hollow and across the plain
to the wall of the Sacsahuaman, where I would
join them, and as soon as they had gone out
of the hollow and were lost to sight I went
to the hole among the bushes where the hidden
stone was and released the chain and let
the water flow back into its old place, till the
entrance to the Hall of Gold was only the
same dark, stagnant pool that any wanderer
might find at the bottom of the cloven stairway.

Then I strewed the earth over the hole, and
piled the stones and brushwood round and
over it as before, and went away to join the
others. I found them standing in a group in
one of the angles of the great fortress, and there

O

I spoke to the soldiers again, and told them how much depended, both for themselves and for the country, on their fidelity, promising them peace and prosperity and freedom if they were faithful, and a speedy death if they betrayed me.

After this I told them what story they should tell when they went back to the city — how their Indian guide had led them into the entrance to a cavern in the mountain, their officer going first and he following, and how, when these two were going on with a single light, some two or three yards ahead of them a great slab of stone had suddenly fallen down between them, closing the passage, and how water had risen up and filled the passage at its lower end, forcing them to run back out of it for fear of being drowned ; and I further gave them permission to bring any who disbelieved them to the mouth of the cleft under the Sayacusca and show them the water that they would find at the bottom of it, but to take good care to send me warning of anyone going there.

This they promised to do, and still full of wonder, and yet pleased with the gold they had got and the promises I had made to them, they made a loyal farewell, and marched down through the Gate of Sand, and went back to the city to tell their story and do the work that I had bidden them do.

When they had gone I sent some of my men to see that none of them turned back, and dismissed the rest to their homes, saving only Tupac, Anahuac, and Ainu and three others who could be trusted in all things; and with these we went back into the underground chambers of the fortress by the way that we had left them.

When we got back to the throne-room I sent all but Tupac away to remove the beasts from the stables and take them to the hacienda, so that the next night, under cover of the darkness, they could return and bring us food and drink and clothing and other things that we needed, for now that matters had gone so far it would not be safe for us to live at the hacienda or be seen in any place known to the Spaniards until the time was ripe for the striking of the first blow.

When they were gone we ate and drank a little of what we had brought with us in the morning, and then lay down, either to sleep or to think of the strange things that had happened and of what was now quickly coming to pass.

As for me, no sleep came to my eyes, for I knew that when Joyful Star awoke I should have to tell her at least something of what her brother had done and of what had happened to him, and a grievous task it was, you may be sure, when I came to the doing of it, as I did not many hours afterwards.

The first thing she asked me when she found that Djama was not with us was what had become of him, and then, knowing that sooner or later the bitter truth had to be told, I told her as gently as I was able, and hiding from her all that I could without lying to her. My words struck her dumb with horror and amazement, and if it had not been that Francis Hartness and the professor were there, and told her that they had seen and heard with their own eyes and ears the truth of all that I said, I do not think she would have believed me. But when at last she could no longer doubt the story of her brother's crime and treachery, she came to me and laid her hand upon my arm, and looked up at me with tearful eyes and said,—

'But you will not kill him, Vilcaroya, for my sake, will you? He is my brother, you know, after all, though he has made me almost ashamed to say so. You must protect yourself, of course, and your people from treachery, but you will not kill him, will you?'

'He is alive now,' I said, 'because he is Joyful Star's brother, not because I think he is worthy to live, for he would have betrayed one life that he gave back, and stained the other with infamy. But I have given my word, and he shall live, and when he can do no more harm I will pardon him, and he shall go back to his own country in safety. More than that I cannot promise even to you.'

'It is all that I can ask for,' she said, 'and more than he could expect after what he has done. But, oh! why should he have brought such a shame as this upon us?'

'Upon himself only,' I said. 'It would not be possible for such a thing as shame to touch you.'

She looked up at me again and smiled through her tears, as if my words had pleased her well, and that smile of hers was more to me than even her tears. Then she went back to the little chamber where she had slept, and presently returned leading Golden Star by the hand, and then we all sat down in the silver seats and talked of the wonderful things that had happened, and I told Golden Star all the story of my own return to life, and hers, and what I knew of the changes that had happened in the world since she and I had said our last words to each other in the Sanctuary of the Sun ; and then I set her talking with the others, translating for her and for them as well as I could, and she, knowing nothing of what had happened in the night, and being glad that Evil Eyes, as she called Djama in our own speech, had gone away for a long time, was as happy as a child amongst us, and soon even Ruth became more cheerful and began to try and make her say words of English and repeat her name and the professor's and Francis Hartness's after her, for she already loved her dearly, and, even in the midst of her own sorrow, she was rejoiced that the soul which had slept had been so happily re-awakened in her.

After this, Francis Hartness and I began to talk our plans over again, and to discuss the chances of the revolt in Cuzco, and I showed him how, with the help of my people, I would the next day cut off all communication between the valley and the rest of the country until our work was finished there, for I was determined that the first part of the empire of my fathers' that I would re-take should be the City of the Sun itself and the region that it commanded, since I knew that my people still looked upon it as the most sacred spot on earth, and would fight better to take it than any other place. And in this plan Francis Hartness, looking at the matter as a soldier, also agreed with me.

We thought it best that none of us should show ourselves in the open that day, for we knew not

what the effect of the soldiers' story and their
return without their officer might be in Cuzco, for
if it had become widely known, it would certainly
bring many people up to the Rodadero to behold
the scene of so strange an occurrence. So we
spent the day in conversation, and, which was
more interesting to my companions, in exploring
the maze of chambers and passages and winding
galleries which the labour of many thousands of
men had wrought out of the solid rock in the
days of my ancestors, for you must know that in
those days the fortress of the Sacsahuaman was
crowned with a great palace, which was the
strongest place in all the Land of the Four
Regions, and so here were stored very great
treasures, not only of gold and silver and precious
stones, but also weapons and armour and most
finely-woven cloths of the purest wool of the
Vicuña, which is softer than silk, brilliantly dyed
and embroidered with gems and threads of gold,
and the imperial robes that had been worn by
twenty generations of Incas, many sets of each,
since nothing that had belonged to one Inca
might ever be used by another after his death.

Among these were found many sets of the
royal robes of the Coyas or queen-wives of the
Incas, and I took Golden Star aside and told her
to take two of these and to clothe herself in one
and Joyful Star in the other, so that we might

see our two Inca princesses side by side as they might have looked in the days of the past, and she fell in with my humour, laughing and clapping her hands like a delighted child.

So she took the robes and led Joyful Star away with her to their own chamber, talking to her in her soft, musical speech, though she knew she could not understand her, and yet making so many pretty signs and eloquent gestures that Ruth, forgetting her sorrow for the time, comprehended her, and entered into the spirit of the play, and soon they came back to us into the throne-room, clad exactly alike, and so perfectly resembling each other, save for the contrast of the blue eyes and the brown, and the bright hair and the dark, that they could have been taken for nothing save twin daughters of the Sun and the fairest of his children; and Tupac and the two men that I had kept in the fortress to attend to our wants fell on their knees before them as they passed, as though they would have worshipped them.

It was at this time, and while we were passing the hours in this fashion, that Golden Star did something that gave me great joy and a bright hope for the future. I had been telling her of the wonderful country that I had returned to life in, and of the marvellous things that I had seen there, and this, she knew already, was the country of Francis Hartness. So, as he came from such a wonderful land, she thought, in the innocence of her old-world simplicity, that he was one of a new race of beings that came on to the earth since our days, and when I told her he was but human like ourselves, though very strong and learned and skilled in many things that we knew nothing of, she said to me, just as a sister might say to a brother from whom she had no secrets,—

'He is rather, in my eyes, like a son of our Father who has come to earth from the Mansions of the Sun; yet I am very glad that he is not, and that he is a man such as you are, my brother, and when Joyful Star has taught me the speech of her people I will talk with him, and then I think life will be better for me, for even now, though I cannot understand his words, his voice sounds like music to me, and when he looks at me he makes me try to remember something that was in my other life, and I have forgotten. What is it, I wonder?'

I looked down into her eyes and saw the untroubled serenity of her soul reflected in them. There was no flush on her cheeks, and her lips were smiling as they could not have smiled had she known how I could have answered that question for her. I stooped and kissed her brow and said,—

'I might guess what it is, Golden Star, but I could not tell you. Yet I pray that our Father the Sun may put it into the heart of my friend to teach you what I see now you can only learn from him.'

More than this I would not tell her, though she questioned me sharply. But the next time that Francis Hartness spoke to her through my lips she looked up at him, and a little flush came to her cheeks, and a smile to her lips, and I saw his eyes brighten, and the colour deepen ever so little under the bronze of his skin.

Then I looked at Joyful Star and saw something shining in her eyes too, and as she caught my glance she smiled ever so little and said, when I had finished speaking for him,—

'Vilcaroya is an excellent interpreter, I've no doubt; but don't you think, Captain Hartness, it would be very much more interesting if you could talk directly with Her Highness? You know I'm teaching Golden Star English, and Vilcaroya is teaching you Quichua — now, I wonder which of you will be able to talk to the other first?'

He pulled his moustache and laughed, looking at Golden Star the while, and said,—

'Well, Her Highness has the advantage of the easier language and the freshest, and I daresay the brightest intellect, but probably for all that we shall begin with some delightful jargon of both languages, and leave them to sort themselves out as we go on. Still, as you say, it will be more interesting than talking through an interpreter.'

'And I hope,' she said, with more meaning in her voice than in her words, 'that you will both of you find it as pleasant as it will be interesting.'

'Who knows!' he said, catching her meaning and laughing again. 'She is most wonderfully like you, Miss Ruth, isn't she?'

'Yes, but—but I am not without hope that you may some day compare us a little, just a little, to my disadvantage.'

What Francis Hartness would have said to this I cannot say, though I do not think he was displeased by Joyful Star's words, and yet his face grew very serious as she spoke. But just then Tupac came and told me that Anahuac and Ainu had returned with the beasts, and were now waiting outside the bronze doors. From this we learnt that it was already night, though, truth to tell, the time had passed so quickly for us that I for one thought that it was little more than late afternoon.

Now, as I have said, I was the only one who knew the secret of the bronze doors, and so I went back with Tupac and opened them, and, when the men had entered, closed them again.

There were twelve of them beside Ainu and Anahuac, and all were laden with food and drink and clothing, and our arms and ammunition, two repeating rifles and two revolvers for each of us. When the men had laid their burdens down, I called Anahuac to me, and asked him if he had any news. He bowed himself before me, and then, standing in front of me as I sat in one of the seats, he said,—

'Yes, Lord. If the ears of the Son of the Sun are open, his servant will fill them with tidings of some moment.'

'Say on,' I said, 'and meanwhile let a meal be prepared for us, for we are hungry.'

This I said to Tupac, and Golden Star, hearing it, smiled, and took Ruth's hand and led her to the boxes, making signs that they should perform the housewife's duties together. Then Anahuac began, and said,—

'The ears of the Children of the Blood have not been closed, nor have their eyes slept throughout the Holy City and the Valley of the Sun, and they have seen and heard much, and the courage of their hearts has risen high, and they are longing for the word of their

Lord to break the yoke that is upon their necks.

' When the soldiers returned last night and told the story that my Lord had put into their mouths, there was great wonder among all the other soldiers, and many saw in it a sign that the Son of the Sun is mighty, and can do that which he promises. But among the masters who are set over the soldiers there was great anger, and they sought, but without avail, to keep the news from being made public in the city ; but the Men of the Blood took care that this should not be so, and to-day all Cuzco has been talking of the strange fate of the Coronel Prada, the son of Don Antonio Prada, the governor. But Don Antonio himself had gone the day before to a hacienda near Oropesa, and messengers have been sent to him to tell him the story, and this evening he rode back with all haste to the city.

' He has ordered that to-night sentries shall be posted at all the approaches to the Rodadero and round the Sayacusca, so that none may come or go without his knowledge, and to-morrow he will come himself with many officers and two hundred soldiers, and the thing they call dynamite, that he may rend the Sayacusca in pieces, and find, as he thinks, the place where his son has been hidden.'

'And the soldiers—what of them?' I asked. 'Will they be for us or against us?'

'There will be many in the service of my Lord, and if it shall be possible there shall be more of these than of the others, for those who were in the Hall of Gold last night have been busy in the hope of my Lord's further bounty, and many have been tempted with the promise of gold and freedom; but still there will be many that may not be trusted, and all the officers of the Governor will be Spaniards.'

'And therefore enemies,' I said, when he had finished his story, and stood waiting for me to speak.

I told Francis Hartness at once what Anahuac had said, and we debated for a short time on what we should do. Then I called Tupac, and he came and stood beside Anahuac, and I said to them,—

'These things have happened well for us, and now we must act quickly, so that we may take the best advantage of them. When you go hence, take with you twenty strips of the scarlet fringe in token of my authority, and give these to twenty of the best of the Men of the Blood, and let them go with all speed and silence through the towns and villages of the valley, and say that the Son of the Sun has come, and is about to stretch forth his hand and take that which was his again. Further, let every entrance to the valley be closed. Let the bridge over the Great Speaker be cut with all speed that may be. Let none pass in or out of the gateway of Piquillacta, and let all the mountain paths be broken down or blocked, so that none may know what is happening in the valley, nor any news be carried hence into the country.

'Let every hacienda, whose master is a Spaniard, be given to the flames, but let no one else be injured. Let none of the strangers be hurt, and let their goods be sacred. Let all of the sentries who will not serve us be disarmed or slain silently by the others, and this before midnight, and let those who are for us —who shall come with the Governor to-morrow —make ready to do quickly that which shall be commanded them. The password for those who are with us will be "Vilcaroya." The rest I will do with my own hands and the help of my friend. I have spoken—let me be obeyed quickly!'

Then they bent low before me and went to make ready to do what I had bidden them.

It was then about eight o'clock at night, and after we had had our evening meal we waited until it was nearly eleven, making perfect our plans, and then, when Ruth and Golden Star had gone to rest without knowing of the work which we had in hand—for we had kept it from them lest they should be anxious for us—Francis Hartness and I armed ourselves, after I had disguised him as well as I could to make him look like an Indian, and we said good-night to the professor and left the fortress by the same way that we had left it the night before.

As soon as we got out into the open air we made our way stealthily back towards the Rodadero, until I caught sight of a sentry standing near one of the carved stones.

'I will go and see whether this is a friend or a foe,' I whispered. 'Wait here and cover him with your rifle, but do not fire unless you hear me whistle.'

'Very well,' he said; 'but take care of yourself, for those Mannlicher bullets make a very ugly wound.'

I waved my hand to him in reply, and went away towards the sentry, keeping a good lookout for others who might be about. I had in my belt a long, heavy-bladed knife, and this I loosened in the sheath as I came near to him. I got within earshot of him unseen, and then, rising to my feet behind him, I said in a low voice, but loud enough for him to hear,—

'Vilcaroya—friend or foe?'

'*Halta! quien va?*'

The words in the hated Spanish speech told me that he was a foe. As he faced about, bringing his rifle to the ready, I drew my knife and, before he could take aim, sent it whistling through the air with such force and so true an aim that it took him in the windpipe and half buried its blade in his neck. That was one of the tricks of our old warfare which, with many others, I had taken good care not to forget.

He dropped his rifle and clasped his hands to his throat and fell without a sound. I crept swiftly forward, pulled the knife out of his throat and drove it into his heart. Then I quickly took off his cartridge-belt and long coat and cap, and put them on. After that I took his rifle and stood in his place for a little while, so that the others might see me, and then walked back to where I had left Hartness. When he saw me coming, his rifle-barrel moved till it covered me, and he said in English,—

'Is that you, Vilcaroya?'

'Yes,' I said. 'The sentry was an enemy, and I have killed him. Now I am going to take you prisoner, as though I were the sentry, and so we can go together and find the officer who commands the sentries, and take him prisoner or kill him.'

'All right,' he said with a laugh. 'I surrender.

This isn't quite what we call civilised warfare, but I suppose it can't be helped.'

We went back together to the place where the sentry that I had killed had stood, and then we saw two or three others coming in towards the place, no doubt to see why the other sentry should have left his post. I took Hartness's rifle out of his hand, and, catching him by the arm, led him to meet the nearest of them, as though I had taken a prisoner. Within ten paces of them I halted, and said,—

' Is it Vilcaroya or Prada ? '

'Vilcaroya to a friend, Prada to an enemy,' he answered, in the dialect in which I had addressed him.

'Then we are friends,' I said, taking off the peaked cap that had belonged to the other sentry, and showing him the long, straight, brown hair that betokened my race. 'I am he who has come back from the days that are dead—Vilcaroya, the son of Huayna-Capac.'

'And I am thy servant, Lord,' he said, bringing his rifle-butt down between his feet, and bending his head over the muzzle. 'I am one of those who saw the glory of my Lord in the Hall of Gold last night.'

'Then thou art one of the faithful,' I said, 'for none have betrayed the secret or earned the swift death that would have been theirs had they done so. Now tell me, how many of those who are on guard here to-night may be trusted ? '

'There are twenty of us here, Lord, not counting the officer in command.'

'Nay,' I said, interrupting him, 'there are but nineteen, for he who wore this coat and carried this rifle was an enemy, and I have killed him, as I would have killed thee hadst thou been an enemy. Now, of these nineteen, how many may I trust ? '

'There are but five who may not be trusted, not counting the officer, and he is a Spaniard, and must be killed.'

'That is good,' I said, for the tone in which he had said these last words had pleased me well. ' Now this man with me is my faithful friend, and one who will fight well for me and my people. Go on the other side of him, and we will take him as a prisoner to the officer. Then thou shalt see how Vilcaroya deals with his enemies.'

He bent his head in assent, and took his place beside Hartness, and as we marched away Hartness said to me,—

'I don't think I shall have much to teach you in strategy, Vilcaroya, but I must say that I would rather have a stand-up fight than this kind of thing.'

'It is not like what you have told me of the

warfare of the English,' I said, 'yet if it has to be it must be. Let us get it over.'

So we marched him between us across the plain, and when we got between the wall of the fortress and the carved stone that they called the Inca's Seat, we saw the officer who was in command of the sentries walking, with two soldiers beside him, from post to post, seeing that the sentries were awake and keeping proper watch. We went to meet him, and halted ten paces from him at his command. I had told the sentry to reply for me, and he answered the officer's hail and said,—

'Vilcaroya!—a prisoner.'

As the first words left his lips the two soldiers repeated the password and made with their rifles the movement that is called the salute. My knife was already in my hand, and as the officer gave a command in Spanish, it flashed once in the starlight and the next instant was buried to the hilt in his breast. He fell, as the sentry had done, without a cry, for it had smitten him to the heart, dead as though he had been struck by a lightning bolt. The others stared at his fallen body, dumb with amazement, and I heard Hartness utter a sound that might have been one either of horror or of wonder; but I had no time to take heed of this, so I instantly ordered the two soldiers to take the officer's uniform off his body, and then I said to Hartness,—

It had smitten him to the heart.

To face page 228.

'Now, you can speak Spanish and I cannot. Take this Spaniard's uniform and his weapons, and make yourself the officer of the guard, and then you shall help me to set a trap that the Governor shall find it a hard matter to escape from.'

CHAPTER XI

HOW WE TOOK THE CITY OF THE SUN

ALTHOUGH Hartness was a much taller and broader man than the Spaniard, his long, loose overcoat fitted him well enough for the occasion, and when he had put on his shako, and wrapped his scarf about his neck so as to hide his fair beard, he was disguised enough to pass in the darkness for one of the enemy. We now took the two soldiers who had been with the officer and visited all the posts. We found four of the sentries who could not return the password and were therefore enemies. These we disarmed and bound instead of killing them, for I could see that what I had done had pleased my friend but little, though he saw that in such a desperate venture as ours it was necessary to use desperate measures.

When we had gone the rounds and made sure of all, we buried the two dead men, and took our prisoners into one of the caves under the carved stones. Then I posted my men so as to guard all the approaches from the city to the Rodadero, and after that I went with Hartness to the hidden hole by the Sayacusca, and showed him how the way to the Hall of Gold was opened. I did this so that the secret might be in good and safe hands if I should fall in battle, and so that he should be able to properly protect the welfare of Ruth and Golden Star, and fulfil my promises to himself and the professor.

When I had turned the stone and showed him the chain, I pulled it up and supported it as I had done before, only this time I used the carbine which had belonged to the sentry I had killed, and to the stock of this I fastened a long rope which Tupac had hidden there by my orders. This rope I stretched out along the ground, hiding it as well as I could, in a straight line away from the Sayacusca. The end I led into the entrance of one of the many passages or tunnels which ran under the carved stones. By the time I had done this the water had all flowed away, and Hartness said to me,—

'Are you going to leave the entrance to your treasure-house open like that for His Excellency to walk into to-morrow?'

'Yes,' I said, 'but it is only half open. Unless the door below is open too there is no way out or in save this and the channel through which the waters flow, so that His Excellency will not find much down there.'

'I see,' he said, 'a trap, and not one that I should care to see a friend of mine walk into. But you don't mean to drown them all like rats in a hole, do you?'

'I cannot tell that yet,' I said. 'If we can take them alive we may do so, but unless they yield to us they shall yield to the water. Now, everything is ready, and we have only to wait. Come and sleep for a little and I will keep watch, and then I will sleep and you shall watch. It will not be daylight for six hours yet, and we can do nothing more till then.'

We went to the cavern in which I had hidden the end of the rope, and he lay down on the soft, clean sand, and, soldier-like, was fast asleep almost as soon as he had lain down. I left him there, and made the round of the guards and spoke with the men, telling them as much as it was necessary for them to know of my plans for the next day, and allowed half of them to take two or three hours' rest, with their arms ready at hand, while the others watched, and then I went back to Hartness and told him to wake me in three hours, and soon was fast asleep in his place. He came and woke me at daylight and told me that everything was still quiet and that the sentries were all in their places.

Then, when we had breakfasted on the food that we had brought with us from the fortress, we called in all the sentries save the two by the Gate of Sand, and hid them among the stones and bushes, all within an easy rifle-shot of the entrance to the water-cavern. I bade the two I had left by the gate tell the Governor that all was well, and, when he had ridden by, to mix with the soldiers and tell those who were for me to separate from the others as soon as they heard my signal-cry, and then to wait for the English captain.

For nearly an hour we sat and watched for the coming of the enemy, and then at last we saw a troop of horse come up out of the valley round the end of the fortress. After them came some officers on horseback, with the Governor riding at their head, and then another troop of horse, in all about three hundred men. The first troop, led by the Governor and his officers, came on towards the Sayacusca, and the others halted and spread themselves out along the ridge that runs round it. When they saw the empty hole and the steps leading down into the darkness, they all crowded round, peering down into it. Then two lanterns were lighted and some of them went down.

They had all dismounted from their horses and were indulging their curiosity without suspicion

I waited till they were nearly all in my trap, and then came the moment to close it. My long, wailing cry rang out loud and shrill through the hollow, and was taken up by my men in hiding, and in an instant all was confusion. I heard my name shouted from one to the other, and saw more than half of the troopers in the hollow leave their ranks and gallop away towards the plain. Then I took aim at a trooper who was watching the officer's horses, and fired. The bullet struck his horse, and it reared up and threw him, and then fell and lay kicking on the ground. At this all the others took fright and broke loose and galloped away in all directions. At the same instant the rifles of my men began cracking all round, and saddle after saddle was emptied as the bullets found their marks.

'I'm going to catch one of those horses,' said Hartness suddenly to me, 'then I'll ride out and bring those other fellows up and show them what to do. That'll be more in my line than this sort of work. Good-bye; you will see or hear of me again before long.'

The next moment he was gone, and I had not fired many more shots before I saw him, mounted on one of the officers' horses, galloping through the hollow towards the ridge. All this time none of my men had shown themselves, and the constant stream of shots coming from all sides of them had thrown the Governor's troops into utter confusion.   The officers were shouting orders which no one listened to, the horses were galloping wildly about, rearing and plunging with the pain of their wounds, and many of the soldiers had already taken to flight, believing, in their panic, that the hollow was full of hidden enemies.

We kept up the fire from our hiding-places until we heard shouts and cheers coming from the ridge, and I looked and saw Hartness with a drawn sword in his hand, leading a body of some hundred and fifty troopers down into the hollow.

Now I saw that we should be able to end the battle quickly, so I sent up my signal-cry again and called for my own men to come out.   Then I pulled the rope and released the chain, and ran out towards my men, shouting to them to close round the entrance to the water-cavern and shoot all who tried to get out.   Some three or four sought to escape and were shot, and then the rest, seeing my men running at them with the bayonet, and the other troopers coming up, led by a stranger, lost heart, and crowded back into the cleft, firing their revolvers wildly as they went.

The next moment we heard cries of terror

coming up out of the darkness, mingled with the rushing of water, and the Governor, followed by about six of his officers, came leaping up the steps to find a line of bayonets drawn up across the mouth. With the waters surging up behind them, and the bayonets in front of them, there was nothing for them but surrender or death.

Hartness, who had now dismounted, ordered the men to fall back a pace, and, as they did so, he went through the line with his sword in one hand and a revolver in the other, and said to the Governor,—

'Señor, will you yield or go back down yonder?'

'We must yield,' said the Governor, 'since there is no choice. But who are you, and what are you, an Englishman, doing here in arms against the Government?'

'Who I am matters nothing just now,' he replied, 'and as for your Government, it no longer exists. That must be enough for you. Now, señores, give up your swords and revolvers quietly and no harm shall come to you. You, Señor Prada, give your sword to this caballero here, who is the Inca Vilcaroya and lawful ruler of this country.'

The Governor turned and stared at me, dumb with amazement at these strange words, and all the others stared too, for, like him, they had no doubt heard the legend of my strange fate. He drew his sword, and as he did so I covered him with my revolver, and extended my hand to take it. He held the hilt out to me with a trembling hand. I took it in silence, and then I turned from him and said to my men,—

'Bring these Spaniards out and bind them safely, then follow me to the Seat of the Incas.'

When they saw that the victory was with us, and that the Governor himself was our prisoner, together with many of the chief of his officers, those of the soldiers who had not been for me when they came were glad enough now to secure themselves by shouting my name and obeying my orders, and when I moved away towards the seat, they followed me, laughing and cheering, well pleased to see their hated masters prisoners in their midst.

The great carved rock which is called the Inca's Seat is, as I have already said, a great rounded mass of stone rising up from the plain of the Rodadero, and carved into many seats. On the top there are three broad seats, the middle one higher than all the rest, and it was here that my forefathers had sat to watch the building of the great fortress, and sometimes to give audience to their people.

Now I sat on it, and the soldiers drew themselves up round the rock, with the prisoners in the midst of them, and I spoke to them, and told them freely of the strange things that had happened to me, and how I had come back to the Land of the Four Regions to drive out their oppressors and restore the just and gentle rule of my ancestors. Then I had the Governor brought up and stood before me, and bade Francis Hartness come and sit on my right hand and speak to him for me, and by his lips I told him that unless the city was surrendered to me before evening he and all his officers should die, and all the houses of the Spaniards in the city should be given to the flames and no pity shown to any man, woman or child of them, for as they had treated my people so I had sworn to treat them unless they yielded.

You may think how troubled he was at hearing such words as these, since he knew from what he had seen that there was conspiracy and treachery among his own men, and he had no knowledge of how far this had gone, or which of his men he could trust, and so this man, who but a few hours before had been master of the whole valley, and had looked upon the Indios, as he called them, as little better than slaves, now answered me humbly enough and prayed me not to murder him when he was helpless in my power. And to this I answered him that the blood of my people had been crying out for many generations against his people, and that this was the day not of mercy but of vengeance, and that I would do as I had said unless the city were delivered to me.

Then I descended from the seat and mounted the Governor's horse, and after I had sent a company of twelve men to ride quickly down to the city and go through all the streets, shouting my name as a signal to tell my people that all was well, and that the moment for them to rise against their oppressors had come, I took my place beside Hartness at the head of our little army, and with our prisoners well guarded close behind us we set out on our way back to Cuzco.

As we approached the city we heard the sound of the church-bells being rung wildly, and looking down, we could see the streets and squares full of people, and as we got nearer still we heard the cracking of rifles and the shouts and cries of men in conflict.

' There is either a fight or a riot going on down there,' said Hartness to me, ' and if many of the soldiers remain faithful to the Government there'll be some bloodshed before to-night. Have you any idea how many there are ? '

' There were more than two thousand soldiers in

the city yesterday,' I said, 'and out of these more than half have already taken my gold and sworn faith to me.   Of the rest many are wavering, and when they see we have taken the Governor prisoner I think they will come over.'

'Very likely,' he said; 'but how about those machine - guns in the barracks?   There are three Gatlings and two Maxims, and if they keep those and work them properly they'll just sweep the streets and squares clear, you know.'

'I have promised fifty pounds' weight of gold for each of them,' I said; 'and, more than that, there should be no ammunition for them by this time if what the sentries told us is true.'

'Yes,' he said, 'if we can get hold of that, or even the best part of it, I don't think there will be much danger.   However, as everything depends on that, I think we had better go straight to the Cuartel first.   If we have that we have Cuzco.'

We entered the city by the street of El Triunfo, and made our way straight to the great Plaza. As we rode along three abreast we were greeted by joyful cries from the crowds of Indians who parted to leave a way for us through the midst of them. Tupac and his comrades had done their work well, and all night the people had been thronging into the city from the surrounding country. All the shops and houses of the Spaniards were already shut up, and although none knew the truth of what was happening, all thought that the revolution had already broken out in Cuzco and so had made themselves as safe as they could.

A little way from the entrance to the great square we came upon Tupac at the head of some two hundred of the men of San Sebastian, armed with knives and guns and pistols of all sorts which they had taken during the night from the towns and villages around, where they had been doing the work I had bidden them do. He told me that there were more than a thousand soldiers in the city waiting only for me to show myself to kill their officers and come over to us, and that the others would fight without heart, if they fought at all, now that the Governor was taken—for half of the people of Cuzco were for the Government and half for the Revolution, and so the city would be divided against itself and all would be confusion as soon as the fighting began.

He also told me that the official who is called the Sub-Prefect had brought out two of the machine-guns and had planted them at each end of the terrace in front of the cathedral, and made a proclamation that unless everyone left the streets within an hour he would have them cleared with bullets.

When I told this to Hartness he said,—

'Then we must have those two guns first. Tell Tupac to break his men up into little bands of about half-a-dozen each and send them round into all the streets leading to the square, and tell everyone that isn't armed to keep out of the way if they don't want to get hurt. Then you ride on with the prisoners and a guard of fifty men, and let them be ready to shoot sharply. Tell them to aim at the knees and not to empty their magazines too fast. I'll look after the guns. They won't fire on you for fear of killing the Governor and the rest. Now, forward!'

I did as he said. Tupac's men broke up and disappeared as though by magic. I took the reins of the horse on which the Governor was bound and bade half-a-dozen of my men to do the same with the others. Then two and two we trotted into the square, Tupac running along by my horse's head. It was covered with groups of people all talking and looking and pointing about them, and on the terrace before the cathedral there were two companies of soldiers, one at each end, drawn up behind a machine-gun.

As soon as the people saw me ride in with the Governor bound beside me a great shout went up and many came running towards me, but I waved them back and shouted to them to leave the square and guard all the streets leading into it. I did this so that those who understood me, and were therefore friends, might escape out of harm's way before the guns began to fire.

Then I drew my revolver and put it to the Governor's head and bade Tupac tell him to order the men away from the guns, and that if a shot was fired he should be the first to die.

So, as there was no help for it, he did so, and called to the officers to come down and speak with him, but instead of obeying they shouted some orders to their men and I saw them making ready to fire the guns, for, as we found out afterwards, they were men who would have joined the revolution when it broke out.

But before the guns could be trained on us Hartness's troop swung round into the square. The twenty foot soldiers sent a volley along the terrace, firing low as he had told them, and killing and wounding nearly half of the men at the guns. Then there came a rattling volley from the cavalry and another from my own men, and then, with a great shout and a clattering of hoofs,

Hartness leapt his horse up the steps at the end of the terrace, where the street slopes up nearly level with it at the back by the cathedral, and charged down on the rear of the enemy just as the gun was swung round.

As he did this I led my men round to the other end of the terrace, where I saw that the men had begun fighting among themselves, and thus I knew that some of them were our friends and were seeking to prevent the others from training the gun on us. I halted, and ordered thirty of my men to dismount and take the gun, which they did with very little trouble, for the others, seeing how they were outnumbered, either threw down their arms and ran away, or surrendered. Two of the officers were killed and another one taken prisoner.

Meanwhile Hartness had cleared the other end of the terrace, and taken the other gun after killing nearly every man who had defended it. But scarcely had this been done than we heard the rattle of drums and the sound of bugles, and saw two columns of men marching at the double out of the Plaza Del Cabildo, where the barracks are, and the other past the Church of the Jesuits, which is at the other end of the square.

'Are those friends or enemies, or both?' Hartness asked me, when he had ordered the two guns to be trained, one on each of the columns, and sat down behind one of them himself.

'If there are friends among them,' I said, 'they know what to do, and when they have done it you can fire.'

Even as I spoke the two columns seemed to break up. Scores of men broke out of the ranks, shouting my name and cheering, and these all ran together towards the fountain in the middle of the square. The rest stopped in wonder and confusion, their officers shouting furiously at them, and ordering them to fire on the deserters. Some obeyed, others, when they saw the guns trained on them, ran away and hid themselves in doorways, and then Hartness gave the order to fire.

Instantly every sound was drowned by the terrible voices of the machine-guns. Hartness glanced once along the barrel of his, and then sent a torrent of bullets full into the middle of the broken column that had come down from the Plaza Del Cabildo. Then he moved it a little from side to side, and then stopped. When the smoke had drifted away I saw that there was not a living being in that corner of the square, only huddled heaps of corpses and bodies of animals. Then he turned the gun on the other corner into which the other gun was firing, and soon not a man or an animal was left alive there also.

When the firing ceased there were none left in the square but those who had declared for us. Hartness immediately formed these into two columns. He led one of them, with one gun at the head, into the street past the Church of the Jesuits, and I led the other with the second gun into the other street leading to the Cuartel, and up these two streets we fought our way into the Plaza Del Cabildo, in which we could hear more fighting already going on.

When we at last gained the square we found a furious fight going on in front of the Cuartel between one body of men who were defending the building and another that was attacking it, but which of these were friends or foes we did not know until Tupac, heedless of the flying bullets, ran out shouting in Quichua that Vilcaroya had come. Shouts and cheers from the Cuartel soon told us that our friends had got possession of it, and after the city was won I learned that when the two columns had started, leaving a third drawn up in the square before the Cuartel, those who were for us, remembering what I had said about the gold that I would give for the machine-guns and the ammunition, had broken their ranks and made a rush for the doors to secure the three guns which were in the courtyard, and so the fight had begun, they seeking to hold the Cuartel against the others until help came.

As soon as I knew which were our enemies, by their bullets coming singing about our ears, I had the gun trained on them, and gave the word to fire.   But no sooner had it begun to rain its tempest of death than we heard the other one speak from the other end of the square, and such a storm of bullets swept across the Plaza that before many moments had passed there was not a man or beast left alive in it.

Then, when the firing ceased again, those who had held the Cuartel, and had taken shelter in it as soon as the machine-guns began to play, threw open the doors to us and came out to welcome us, and Francis Hartness and I clasped hands as victors, and for the time being, at least, masters of the ancient City of the Sun, for with the Cuartel we had taken all the arms and ammunition stored up in Cuzco, including the three Gatling guns and the two Maxims; and more than this, the whole of the native population of the valley was in our favour.

The fighting was now over, save for conflicts that were going on in different parts of the city between the Spaniards and the Indians, and I at once had the Governor brought before me in the Cuartel and told him by the lips of Hartness to write a proclamation surrendering the city to us and ordering all the officials to come in and make their submission before sundown, threatening fire and sack to every Spanish house if it was not done. This he did, knowing well what would befall him if he refused. At the same time Hartness made a proclamation in my name in English and Spanish promising perfect freedom and security to all foreign merchants in the region that was under our command.

It was then about mid-day, and when I had given Francis Hartness full authority to act in my name as Governor of the city, which, speaking fluent Spanish as he did, he could do better than I, I took a guard of fifty men and went with Tupac back to the Rodadero, and took ten of the men into the Hall of Gold and bade them carry out as much as they could, so that I might keep my promise to the soldiers who had been faithful to me, and while they were doing this I went with Tupac to Djama's cell and found him wailing and crying like a little child, and beating his hands on the golden wall of his prison and praying most piteously for a sight of the daylight and a breath of the fresh air of heaven.

The Spaniard, when he heard us coming, began to shriek and scream, and I bade Tupac tell him that I would gag him for a day and a night if he did not cease his cries. But to Djama I told what had happened, and how Cuzco was already mine, and promised I would let him out for a little while the next day if he would keep silence for half-an-hour, and hearing this, he ceased his cries, and I went on to the throne-room to take the news of our victory to Ruth and Golden Star.

CHAPTER XII

QUEEN AND CROWN

I FOUND them in the midst of an English lesson which Golden Star was taking, sitting, still clad in her Inca costume, between the professor and Joyful Star, who also was dressed in the same fashion. They all three rose to meet me as I entered the throne-room, and Ruth coming forward with both hands outstretched, as she had never done before, said,—

'What have you been doing all this time, Vilcaroya, and why are you looking so worn and haggard? Have—have you been fighting? And why have you come back here alone?'

'Yes,' I answered, taking her hands into mine, and feeling all my blood turn to flame as their gentle pressure thrilled along my nerves. 'Yes, we have been fighting, and the Lord of Light has fought upon our side, for we have gained the victory, and the city is ours.'

'Thank God for that!' she said; 'and that no harm has come to you—or to Captain Hartness.'

'What! do you mean to say you have taken Cuzco already?' cried the professor. 'How on earth did you manage that so quickly?'

'Because,' I replied, 'as I told you, my father the Sun fought on my side and turned the hearts of his children towards me, and so Francis Hartness led them to speedy victory, and the hearts of our enemies fainted within them, and they have yielded. Now I have come to tell you how it happened, and to take Joyful Star back to the city, where she shall be hailed as queen.'

Then I sat down with them and told them all, from the taking of the Governor and his officers prisoners by the Sayacusca to the capture of the Cuartel and the making of Francis Hartness Governor of Cuzco. After that I went and put on the imperial robes, which I had now a double right to wear, and led them through the gates of bronze into the Hall of Gold.

Now, in the joy of my triumph, and the greeting that Ruth had given me, I had forgotten to bid her keep silence while going through the hall, and when she saw the two cells in the corner built up with blocks of gold she stopped and said,—

'Those were not here the other night. What have you had them built up like that for?'

And before I could answer, Djama's voice, shrill and trembling, rose out of the cell, crying,—

'Ruth, Ruth, I am here! This is my prison. It is a grave of gold. Curse the gold! Save me, save me, Ruth, for I am going mad—and I am your brother!'

She stopped and took hold of my arm with both her hands, and looked up at me. Her face was very pale and her lips were trembling. Yet though her voice was low, it was firm as she said to me,—

'I have no brother who is a liar and a traitor to his friends; but, Vilcaroya, I had a brother once who was very good and kind to me, and for the sake of his goodness and kindness I ask you to treat this—this prisoner of yours more gently.'

'Joyful Star can ask nothing to-day that I could refuse,' I said. 'He shall be taken out forthwith and lodged with all comfort, though I must keep him safely.'

'No, no, not till I am gone!' she whispered, taking Golden Star by the arm and leading her towards the passage. But, softly as she had spoken, Djama heard her, and in his rage and despair at her words he cried,—

'You—you won't see me! But you will go

with your lover, your Indian master, who owes his life to me! You will sell yourself for his gold and be his wife. Oh, my God!—my sister!'

And then he raved in the madness that came upon him, and his voice rang horridly out of his cell and echoed shrilly through the hall and the passages about it. I could feel no anger against a man who was helpless and my prisoner, so I followed Ruth without speaking; and when we stood once more in the sunlight she turned to me with a bright flush on her cheeks and great tears in her eyes, and said very softly and sweetly,—

'He is mad, poor Laurens! he must be. That terrible gold has turned his brain, or he could never speak to me like that. You will not treat him more harshly for it, Vilcaroya, will you, for you know, after all, he is—I mean he was my brother, and I loved him very much—once?'

'Yes, he is mad,' I said; 'and yet the lips of madness may speak truth, for what am I but what he said?'

'Have you forgotten what you asked me, or what I answered when I kissed Golden Star in the throne-room, that you can speak like that?' she said, with one swift glance that told me I had not asked in vain.

What more she might have said I know not,

but she had said enough to set my heart dancing and my blood thrilling with a joy greater than I had found in the speedy conquest of the city of my fathers, and just then Tupac came to me and said that a sufficient quantity of gold had been taken out, and that all was ready to return to the city.   Then I told him what he was to do with Djama and his fellow-prisoner, and ordered Golden Star's litter and the horse for Ruth which we had brought with us to be made ready, and also a mule for the professor, and when Tupac had returned we set out along the road that leads to the Gate of Sand, I riding in the midst of the troop, and Ruth on my left hand and Golden Star in her litter on the right.

As we approached the streets, great crowds of my delivered people thronged out to welcome us, and when they saw me riding on my black horse, dressed in the imperial robes and with the Llautu on my brow, they set up a shout of joy and welcome that went ringing along the streets and through the squares and all over the city, and so I rode on through the bareheaded throngs, who bowed themselves almost to the earth before me.

As we were crossing the great Plaza, Ruth looked about her with bright cheeks and shining eyes and said to me,—

'Is it not all like a dream, Vilcaroya? Only a few weeks ago you came here poor and unknown, and now you are a king come back to your own again. Is it not wonderful?'

'Yes,' I said, looking into her eyes with more courage than before; 'but something more wonderful even than that has befallen me. Is it not so, my queen?'

'Your queen is not crowned yet, your Majesty!' she said, looking down, and yet not frowning, as I half feared she would.

'No,' I answered, ' nor shall she be till my work is done, and the whole land that was my fathers' is mine to give her, and then all that power and gold and love can give her shall be hers.'

'Give me the last and I shall ask no more,' she said softly, chasing with that first sweet confession from my heart the last lingering doubt of the great blessing that my Father the Sun had bestowed upon me.

Thus we came to the front of the Cuartel, where all the troops were already drawn up to do us honour, and Hartness came out to greet us. He stopped for an instant, and his cheeks paled a little as he saw Ruth riding at my side, already dressed as she would be when she was my queen. But then the goodness of his honest heart spoke from his lips, and he said, as he held out his hand to me,—

'Welcome, your Majesty! Majesties, I might almost say, I suppose! The city is ours and everything is quiet. Some of the officials have come in and submitted; others I have had to put under arrest, and runners are coming in every minute from the other towns in the valley to say that our plans have been carried out perfectly. The rest of our work won't be as easy as this has been, but we've made a very good beginning, and, at anyrate, I think I can congratulate your Majesty on having made your two most important captures.

He looked at Ruth as he said this, and though her fair face flushed brightly and her eyes fell, yet she spoke steadily enough when she answered him, saying,—

'You can hardly call me one of the spoils of war, I think, Captain Hartness, though I confess that I have surrendered at discretion. Now give me your hand and help me down, and don't look so disconsolate, for you are not nearly as unfortunate as you think. There is an Inca princess for you also, a real one, too. I have been teaching Golden Star to say your name, and, do you know, she makes it sound just like music with that sweet voice of hers. See, here she is, and you shall hear her say it.'

I had dismounted meanwhile, and taken Golden Star from her litter, and when the people saw her,

her name ran swiftly from lip to lip, and a great shout of delight rose up from thousands of throats to welcome her back to life and the home of her long-dead fathers. Then I took her hand and Hartness's, and put hers in his, and said to him,—

'My friend, what I have taken I can in some measure give back to you. Here is Joyful Star's sister-soul and living likeness. I have seen her newly-awakened soul look out of her eyes with love upon you, as in good truth it well might, for you are a true son of the Sun, though not of our blood. In the days to come you may learn to love her too, and then all will be well.'

'Yes,' said Ruth, coming to his side, 'and better than it could have been in any other way. The very Fates themselves seemed to have arranged all this, so it is not for mortals to rebel, Captain Hartness.'

He looked at her almost sadly for a moment, and then he laughed a little and said,—

'I should be more or less than mortal if I did, Miss Ruth. But mind, if I am faithless, remember it is you who have done the most to make me so.'

As he said this he took Golden Star's little hand in his own and kissed it. As she felt the touch of his lips a new light sprang into her eyes and shone and danced there, and she said to me,—

' Why does the Son of the Great People do that, and what have you said to him about me, my brother ? '

' He has kissed your hand in loving greeting,' I answered, 'and what I have said he will no doubt tell you better some day when you can speak together.'

The bright blood in her cheeks told me that she had understood me, and she turned her head away, but she did not take her hand from Hartness's, and so I gave my hand to Ruth and led her into the Cuartel, and Hartness and Golden Star followed us hand in hand amidst the cheers of the soldiers and the joyful shouts of the people.

That night there were such rejoicings in Cuzco as the City of the Sun had not seen since the Spaniards came into the land. I distributed the gold among the soldiers as I had promised, giving to each man a piece of about two ounces in weight, and they, who had never possessed, even if they had ever seen, gold before, kissed it and fondled it in their delight, and swore that they would fight for me as long as one of them was left alive ; and then I spoke to them and told them that they had but to be faithful and brave, and their English leader would lead them to victory after victory, until the whole land should be ours.

Later on I sent Tupac with many men up to

the fortress, and they brought down the Golden Throne and the symbols of the Sun and great quantities of gold and jewels, and they set the throne in the midst of the terrace in front of the cathedral, with silver seats on either side of it, on the spot where in the olden time stood the Palace of Viracocha; and on the front of the cathedral, over the great doors, they fixed the symbols of the Sun, and high above all, between the two bell-towers, they placed a great flagstaff.

Before daybreak the next morning the square was thronged with people, save for an open space which the soldiers kept before my throne. I took my place amidst an utter silence. Ruth and Golden Star sat on my right and on my left, and Francis Hartness, with a drawn sword in his hand, stood by my throne to the right, and on the terrace behind me, and on either side, stood the Men of the Blood, dressed in their ancient and long-forbidden costumes, with which I had furnished them out of the stores in the secret chambers of the fortress.

No word was spoken and no sound was heard over the whole city, and all eyes were turned to the swiftly brightening eastern sky.

The blue changed to silver and the silver to crimson and gold. Then the sun, the glorious image of the Lord of Life, uprose in all his sudden splendour, and as his rays fell on the great golden jewel-rayed circle on the cathedral front, the Rainbow Banner ran swiftly up to the head of the flagstaff, and I, rising from my throne, bared my head and, turning my face to the rising sun, bowed myself before it, and at the same instant every head in the vast assembly was uncovered, and all, save the soldiers, fell on their knees and stretched out their hands to heaven in silent joy and thankfulness.

Then I lifted up my voice and spoke the ancient Invocation to the Sun which generation after generation of my fathers had spoken from the same spot at the beginning of the feast of Raymi, and when I had ended this the Children of the Blood lifted up their voices after me and sang the long-silenced and yet never-forgotten hymn to the Sun, and then, standing before the kneeling multitude, I replaced the Llautu on my brow and proclaimed myself Inca and supreme Lord of the Land of the Four Regions in the name of my long-dead fathers, whose divine right to lordship had been preserved in me.

And so I, Vilcaroya, son of Huayna-Capac, first fulfilled the prophecy that had been spoken in the Days of Darkness, and so did I come, as had been said, from one life into another through the shadow of death and the silence of the grave, with her whose love, now changed, though no less dear, had nerved me to face the ordeal of the strangest fate that had ever befallen one born in mortal shape.

CHAPTER XIII

HOW DJAMA PAID HIS DEBT

IT is one of the mysteries of this lower life of ours that men, meaning to do good in all honesty of heart, may yet do evil in the doing of it, and it was thus with me in the hour of my first triumph and rejoicing.

I had pondered long and deeply over the strange treachery of Djama, and I had talked of it with Francis Hartness and the professor until I had come to see that he was in truth sorely afflicted with that madness which is born of the lust of gold, which, as they told me, is a disease of the soul that makes timid men rash and mild ones fierce and cunning, and may even turn the gentleness of woman into the pitiless rage of beasts of prey.

It was through thinking of this that I came to see that I was by no means blameless myself

for his madness and the treachery that had
come from it.

In my own days and among my own people
gold was held precious only for its beauty and
its usefulness. We had not learned the art of
making it into money and buying men's souls
and bodies with it, but I had already lived enough
of my new life to see that now, save for the few,
gold was all and honour nothing; and knowing
this, I should also have known what I was
doing when I showed Djama the treasures in
the Hall of Gold. The sight of them had made
him mad, and, as my hand had shown them to
him, the blame of what he had done in his madness was in part mine.

All this I remembered in the hour when my
soul was filled with joy and my heart warm with
love, and I thought how great a pleasure I should
give to her who had given me the better part of
my own joy if I looked upon Djama with pity
and forgiveness and did an act of mercy as the
first deed of my new reign.

So, when the ceremonial of my crowning was
over, I bade Tupac take some of my body-guard
and bring him before me from the place where
he had been lodged after his release from his
golden cell, and at the same time I quieted
the fears of Joyful Star by telling her what
was in my heart concerning him.

They brought him unbound, but well guarded by soldiers with bayonets on their rifles, up the broad avenue which the parted throng had made across the square in front of my throne.

I saw him stare wildly about him as he came near, gazing at the splendid sun-lit pageant like a man in a dream, or one just awakened into another world, as I had been after my long death-sleep. But when he came near, and saw me sitting in my royal state with Joyful Star on my right and Golden Star on my left, both robed as princesses of the Ancient Blood, his face grew dark with passion, and his eyes, losing their wonder, gazed in fixed and furious hate at me — the man who was going to give him his life, and much more that he had coveted besides.

They placed him between two soldiers before me at the foot of the terrace steps above which my throne had been set, and I was about to speak and greet him kindly, when his anger already got the better of him, and, with a mocking smile on his lips, he said in a loud, rough voice that was most unlike his own quiet, even tones,—

'Well, your Majesty, as I suppose you think yourself for the present, I expected something like this—to be brought out into the midst of your fellow-savages and sentenced like a felon

before my own sister and the woman who, like
yourself, owes her life to me!'

Then he laughed one of his strange, joyless
laughs, and went on before I could reply,—

'Well, I suppose I mustn't grumble. You
have won, and to the victor go the spoils.
Now that you have apparently bought the girl
who was once my sister with your gold, and
I have given you your own sister-wife back,
you will be able to try an interesting experiment in your old form of matrimony—'

I saw Joyful Star shrink back in her seat
and turn her head away from him with a little
cry as he said these evil words, and they
angered me so, that — forgetting they were
spoken by a man who stood helpless before
me—I cried,—

'Silence, liar and speaker of evil! or your
next words shall be the last that human ears
shall hear you speak. Are you still mad, or
have you forgotten that you were once a man?'

He smiled such a smile as you may have
seen on the lips of one who has died in agony,
and said with a swift change in his voice,—

'I beg your Majesty's pardon, and—and the
ladies' too. It was a most ungentlemanly thing
to say, and one should not forget one's manners
on the threshold of the next world—if there
is one. But come, your Majesty, you are

wasting your valuable time, and keeping all these interesting savages of yours waiting. You'll find I shall take it quietly enough. What do you propose that it shall be—something with boiling oil or red-hot pincers in it?'

I knew that a man who could speak thus, believing that he was about to die, must be in a pitiful plight, and so I answered him sternly, and yet without anger,—

'Laurens Djama, I have not brought you here to jest with you, nor yet, as you think, to condemn you to die, though your life is justly forfeit to me and my people, whom you would have betrayed again to their oppressors. Now, listen! You brought me back from death to life, and for my life I will give you yours, and for Golden Star's I will pay you the price agreed on and something more. It was by my foolish act that the madness of the gold-hunger came upon you, and for that I will give you your freedom; but not now, for that would not be safe for me or my people, since you have betrayed us once, and, knowing what you do, might do so again. You shall be taken hence to a pleasant and fertile valley, where you shall have all freedom, save permission to leave it until this war is over and I am undisputed lord of the land of my fathers. Then you shall take the wealth that shall be

yours and go to your own country, or where-
ever you please, so long as you do not remain
in mine, for here there is no place for you,
since my people do not forgive as easily as I
do. Now I have spoken; if there is anything
more that you can ask, and I can give with
safety, ask it.'

Most men who had sinned as he had done
would have very willingly taken such forgiveness, and Laurens Djama might have taken it
but for a seemingly small thing. While I was
speaking to him his eyes had wandered from
mine and were looking into Golden Star's. As
I ceased I felt her hands clasping my arm, and
heard her voice say tremblingly in our own
tongue,—

'Save me, my lord and brother, save me!
Evil Eyes is looking into my heart and turning it cold!'

This Djama saw, though he did not understand her words, and the sight brought the madness into his blood again. He shouted with a
voice like the cry of a wild beast in pain,—

'Curse you! I will have neither life nor
liberty from you, but I'll have your life for mine,
and that will pay me better!'

As the last word left his lips he made a movement so quick that my eyes could not follow it.
.The next instant he had wrenched the rifle from

the hands of the soldier on his right hand and levelled it at me.   Even as he did so Joyful Star flung herself with a scream upon my breast and Hartness sprang forward from behind my throne-seat.

The rifle flashed.   I heard a hissing sound close to my ear and a deep groan and the fall of a body behind me.   In the same moment Djama was seized and flung to the ground, where he lay quite still and silent.   I rose to my feet, clasping Joyful Star for the first time in my arms, and looked round.   Hartness stood beside me unharmed, but old Ullulo, the first friend that I had made in my new life among my own people, lay dead behind my throne with a bullet through his forehead.

I had not forgotten that old training which taught an Inca warrior to look on near-approaching death with unmoved eyes and unshaken heart, and this was only such a hazard as I had taken a score of times before.   I bade Hartness lead Ruth and Golden Star into the temple behind us, so that they should not see what was about to be done.   Then I took my place on the throne again and ordered Djama to be raised and stood on his feet.

He rose of himself, very pale but calm and strong in his own evil strength, fearing nothing, as became a man for whom death had no terrors and, it might be, few secrets. We looked each other in the eyes in silence, and in the midst of an utter stillness that had fallen on the vast throng, until Hartness came back. Then I said,—

'That is enough, Laurens Djama. Choose now what death you will die, but, for your own sake and Joyful Star's, choose a quick one.'

Although my voice was as the voice of doom to him, yet he did not quail even then, for if his heart was black it was very strong, and fear had never entered into it. He drew himself up to the full height of his stature and, looking me full in the eyes, he said as quietly as I had ever heard him speak,—

'That choice is always mine, whether you give it to me or not. You have threatened me with death before and I have told you that you could not kill me. Now watch and see if I spoke the truth.'

Then, with a soldier holding each of his arms and two others grasping his shoulders, he drew a quick, deep, gasping breath. The blood rushed into his face till its pallor became purple. The next instant it became deathly white again. His jaw dropped, his eyes grew fixed and blindly staring, and then his shape seemed to shrink together like an empty bag, and he sank down between those who were holding him.

They pulled him upright again, and his head dropped forward on his breast. He was dead—dead as though the Llapa itself had struck him—and so Laurens Djama, master of the arts of life and death, passed out of the world of living men by the act of his own will, though not of his own hand.

CHAPTER XIV

Now this story of mine is nearly done, for there are but few things left for me to tell. It is not for me to write of all the battles that we fought after the City of the Sun and the region about it fell into our hands, for to do that is a task better fitted to the hands of him who led my ever-growing hosts to victory after victory until the whole land that had been my fathers' was mine from north to south and from the great rivers of the east to the Sea of the Setting Sun, which you now call the Pacific Ocean.

It is enough for me to say that I used my gold without stint, and that it did all and more than the work I had been told it would do. As we marched southward and westward to the sea, army after army left those who were fighting between themselves for the ruins of the land

and, having no real quarrel of their own, ranged themselves under the Rainbow Banner and fought with me for freedom and the ancient faith of their long-dead fathers, and how city after city welcomed me as I came to give it peace and wealth instead of strife and misery.

My unforgotten story and the marvel of my coming back from the days of our old-time glories had sped like the leaps of the lightning from mountain to mountain and valley to valley, and every man in whose veins flowed even the smallest drop of the Sacred Blood threw aside the broken fragments of the oppressor's yoke and came to give me his service.

From other countries, too, and from far over the sea, there came men to fight for me, men whom Hartness had called from afar by speaking to them over the lightning-wires, and they brought ships with them, armed with flame and thunder, which the promise of my gold had purchased, and these took all the seaports for me, while my ever-growing armies were taking the cities of the inland valleys — all of which those who would learn may read in the great book which Francis Hartness and the professor, who with Joyful Star have helped out these lame words of mine, are writing together to tell how the ancient empire of the Incas rose at my call

and the bidding of my gold — which I doubt
not was far stronger than I—out of the degradation into which the oppressors had cast it,
and has even now begun to prosper again with
more than its former glory.

But, as I have said, these things are not for me
to tell, since I have neither the skill nor the knowledge to do so. What I have set down here is
only the story of my own awakening out of the
death-sleep into which the arts of the priests of
the Sun had cast me with Golden Star, and of
her return to join me in my new life. I have
told of that and of all that befell us afterwards, and now there remains only the telling
of that which fulfilled our strange fates and
completed our happiness in the new world into
which those fates had brought us.

Many weeks passed and grew into months
before the oppressors were finally subdued and
I found myself undisputed lord of all the land,
and, as I had promised Joyful Star, all this had
to come to pass before I would ask her to put
her hand into mine and take her place beside
me as my Coya and queen on the throne of
Huayna-Capac.

But at length there was peace in the land and
we returned from Lima, the capital of the Spaniards,
where I had been proclaimed and acknowledged
Inca and Emperor of my ancient domains, to

the City of the Sun, which many loving and willing hands had cleansed of the abominations of its new idolatries and made in some measure fit to receive us, to crown our new lives with such happiness as, with the help and blessing of the Unnameable, we might be able to bestow upon each other.

The treasures of gold and silver and ornaments of jewels, the rich hangings and the sacred and precious emblems had been brought from the Hall of Gold and the throne-room beneath the Sacsahuaman and set up in the chief temple of the Spaniards, which stands in the place where the holy Temple of the Sun once stood and is in great part built of the self-same stones.*

It was the eve of the Feast of Raymi, or the Coming of the Sun, which in the olden time we counted as the beginning of the year, and I had determined that this day should witness the restoration of the old order and the beginning of my own true happiness — so that night Golden Star and I, as became the son and daughter of the Royal Race and Sacred Blood, watched and prayed according to the ancient

---

* This is not quite correct, although a natural mistake on the part of the Inca. It is not the Cathedral of Cuzco, but the Church of Santo Domingo, which stands on the site of the ancient Temple of the Sun. It is by far the finest church in Cuzco. The Cathedral faces the great square.

rites—she in a chamber of what had once been the House of the Virgins of Sun, and I in the purified temple—from the setting of the sun until the first waning of the stars in the coming dawn.

Very early in the morning she was brought to me in the temple by Tupac-Rayca—whom I had in virtue of his pure blood and noble decent, consecrated Villac-Umu or High Priest of the Sun, and who had in turn invested such others of the Blood as he thought worthy with the subordinate dignities of the holy office. He and his attendants were arrayed in the ancient priestly robes and adorned with the sacred emblems of their rank, and Golden Star was attired as a royal Virgin of the Sun, in garments of white edged with scarlet and decked with ornaments of pure gold.

Then we prayed together before the newly-set-up altar, which stood over against the eastern window of the Sanctuary, and when that duty was ended, and while the growing light was yet dim, there came to us Joyful Star, also arrayed as a princess of the Blood, and Francis Hartness, whom my thankful people had already named Viracocha, after one of our golden-haired hero-gods of the olden time.

After them came all those of the Sacred Race that were left in the land—men and matrons, youths and maidens—all dressed in the long-forbidden garb of their forefathers, and ranged themselves in two silent, orderly ranks down the sides of the Sanctuary, waiting with patient eagerness for that which they had been bidden here to see.

Above the altar hung the great golden Emblem of the Sun, upon which the radiant glance of the Lord of Light would first fall through the circular window in the eastern wall, and on it was a pyramid of wood anointed with scented oils; for here was soon to be re-kindled—if our Lord the Sun should smile on the new fortunes of his long - suffering children—without the aid of human hands, that sacred fire first lit by Manco Capac and Mama Occlu, son and daughter of the Sun, and which had burnt un-quenched through all the ages that had passed from the founding to the fall of our ancient empire. Beside it lay a cone-shaped vessel of burnished gold, in the depths of which the Sacred Fleece awaited the touch that was to change it into flame.

When all were assembled, Tupac-Rayca mounted the steps of the altar, and, facing the silent throng, began to speak in the ancient and unforgotten tongue and said,—

'Children of the Sun, sons and daughters of those whose ancestors in the unremembered days received the divine command to create the empire over which they ruled with ever-growing glory until, by the inscrutable decrees of the Unnameable, the destroyer and oppressor were permitted to come into the land, listen with open ears and thankful hearts to the words which our Father shall put into my mouth to say to you!'

All bowed their heads and crossed their hands over their breasts as he spoke, and after a little silence he went on,—

'The last of the Villac-Umus who stood where I am standing told your fathers and mine of the near-approaching night of gloom and desolation that was about to fall upon the Land of the Four Regions. For what sins of his children our Father permitted that night to eclipse the bright day of their empire we know not, nor is it lawful for us to inquire. Let it be enough for us to believe that, grievous as the doom was, it could not have been anything save the inflexible justice of the Unnameable.'

Again they bowed their heads, and there was silence for a little space until he went on, speaking this time in a gladder voice,—

'But, stern as that justice was, it was yet not untempered with mercy, for with the words of doom there came from our Father, by the lips of his minister, the holy Anda - Huillac, those words of hope and promise which from that day to this have been handed down in secret, yet unforgotten, from father to son and from mother to daughter, and which now for the first time since then may be spoken openly in the land :—

'" *To that Son of the Sacred Race who, for honour aud faith and love, shall take the hand of a pure virgin of his own holy blood and with her pass fearless through the gate of death into the shadows which lie beyond, shall be given the glory of casting down the oppressor and raising the Rainbow Banner once more above the Golden Throne of the Incas. On that throne he shall sit, and wield power and mete ont justice and mercy to the Children of the Sun when the gloom that is now falling upon the Land of the Four Regions shall have passed away in the dawn of a brighter age.*"

'Sons and daughters of the long-dead, turn your eyes and see how the eastern skies are swiftly brightening with first rays of that long-looked-for dawn. This is the morning of our deliverance, for our deliverers stand here before us, and with your own eyes you may look upon those who, in the strength of their love and faith, dared the doom to win the promise, for here in the living flesh stands that Vilcaroya, son of the great Huayna‑Capac, and there beside him is Golden Star, that virgin of the Royal Race who of her own will joined hands with him in the wedlock of death, and whose pure soul has dwelt with his in the Mansions of the Sun while ten generations of men have lived and died awaiting their return to the land.

'To us, more blessed, it has been given to see that which our fathers waited for in vain. To us our Lord Vilcaroya and our Lady Golden Star have come back from the shadows of death into the light of life and glory of victory. Already you have seen the oppressor pay the price of life for life, and blood for blood, and shame for shame. You have seen our Lord seated on the golden throne of the Divine Manco with the Rainbow Banner waving high above him, and now the moment has come for you to see the fulfilling of what yet remains of the promise unfulfilled. Behold the visible presence of our Father comes near to smile once more on his children long left in darkness!'

While he was speaking these last words the light in the eastern sky had brightened fast until a sunray leapt over the lower rim of the window and shone on the painted ceiling of the Sanctuary. At a sign from Tupac-Rayca,

Golden Star took up the vessel in which lay the Sacred Fleece, and, standing in the middle of the altar on the highest step, held it poised in her hands above her head, with her pale, fair face and shining eyes upturned towards the window.

Foot by foot the light crept along the roof, broadening and brightening as it went, till it touched the western wall. Then, ever followed by the anxious eyes of the silent throng, it descended until the great Symbol of the Sun flashed and flamed in its radiance. Still lower it sank and the burnished vessel that Golden Star held to receive them caught the gathering rays and glowed as though filled with liquid fire.

Now the moment for the giving of the Sign had come. A faint wreath of pale blue smoke curled upwards from the Sacred Fleece. It grew darker and denser, and then a little tongue of flame leapt out from the midst of it. At the same instant Tupac seized the vessel and held it upturned over the pyramid of wood upon the altar. The burning fleece fell down upon the anointed wood, a long shaft of fire shot upward, and, as the descending sunrays fell over the face and bosom of Golden Star, the voice of Tupac rang out in an exultant chant through the silence, saying,—

Now the moment for the giving of the Sign had come.

To face page 280.

' Rejoice, Children of the Sun, rejoice! for your Father has once more looked in kindness and blessing upon you, and with the radiant glance of his eyes he has re-kindled the long-quenched fire which henceforth shall burn upon his altar as long as his visible presence shall make bright the heavens and beautiful the earth!'

As he ceased, Golden Star's voice rose up clear and sweet, singing the first words of the Hymn to the Sun—as I alone of all that throng had heard her sing them in the days that were no more. Then the Children of the Blood raised their voices too, and out of the fulness of their thankful hearts poured forth their first tribute of praise and thanksgiving to Him who had broken the yoke of the oppressor and given back light and joy and peace to the long-darkened Land of the Four Regions.

When the Hymn to the Sun was ended and the Children of the Blood had received the blessing of Tupac, there was yet one more ceremony to be performed before the rejoicings of the Feast of Raymi began. There is little need for me to tell you what it was. In love as in war I had striven and conquered, and now the dearest of my rewards, dearer far than wealth or empire, was to be made mine by

T

the free gift of her who was herself that which she gave.

Two of the priests brought forth the marriage-font and placed it in front of the altar, and Joyful Star stood on the one side of it and I on the other and we joined hands across it.

It was a double vessel of gold, formed of two twin cups, and between them there was a hole stopped by a golden plug, to which a little chain was fastened. The cup on my side was filled with blood-red wine and that towards Joyful Star with pure water, crystal clear.

Tupac took our hands in his and parted them, saying as he did so,—

'To meet and to part is the lot of man and woman upon earth, yet when two true souls meet and two faithful hearts are joined even death can part them but in seeming, for in the bright halls of the Mansions of the Sun they shall dwell for ever in the blessed presence of our Father!'

So saying, he joined our hands again, and drawing out the golden plug, he pointed to the mingling fluids and went on, speaking now to each of us in turn,—

'Here, Vilcaroya Inca, and you, Joyful Star, daughter of a conquering race and well-beloved of our Lord, see the emblem of the union between you!   As the strong red wine colours and strengthens the pure water, so, Joyful Star, shall the stronger nature of thy chosen husband colour and strengthen thine, and, as the pure water tempers and purifies the wine, so, Vilcaroya Inca, shall the gentler and purer nature of her who is henceforth thy wife and queen by the rites of our ancient law, soften and purify thine according to the will and purpose of the Un-nameable, who to this end sent man and woman upon earth that together they might possess and enjoy it, each helping the other, man making the world fruitful and beautiful by his labour, and woman sweetening his toil by the reward of her love and her constancy.'

Then he raised his hands above our heads as we bowed them together over the emblem of our mingling lives, and said again,—

'Son and daughter, man and wife, who have met from afar, and who in this solemn act have sworn in the all-pervading presence of the Unnameable to lead each other from this your meeting-place to the dim border of the shadow-land which lies between this world and the threshold of the Mansions of the Sun, may the blessing of our Father clothe your brows with honour and fill your hearts with everlasting love and trust, and may He guide your feet to walk in pleasant places from now even to the end!'

As he ceased our hands parted, only to meet again a moment later after we had stepped aside to yield up our places at the marriage-font to Francis Hartness and Golden Star.

THE END

Colston and Coy. Limited, Printers, Edinburgh

F. V. WHITE & Co.'s
Catalogue of Publications

ALEXANDER (Mrs)

A Golden Autumn. 6/-.
What Gold Cannot Buy. 2/6 & 2/-.
A Choice of Evils. 2/6 and 2/-.
Found Wanting. 2/6 and 2/-.
Por His Sake. 2/6 and 2/-.
A Woman's Heart. 2/6 and 2/-.

ALLEN (GRANT)

A Splendid Sin. 6/-.

ARMSTRONG (Mrs)

Letters to a Bride. 2/6.
Good Form. 2/-, cloth.

BEAVAN (ARTHUR H.)

Marlborough House and its Occupants, Present and Past. With 16 full-page Illustrations. 6/-.

CAMERON (Mrs LOVETT)

Two Cousins and a Castle. 3/6.
Little Lady Lee. 2/6 and 2/-.
A Soul Astray. 2/6.
A Bad Lot. 2/6 and 2/-.
A Tragic Blunder. 2/6 and 2/-.
A Bachelor's Bridal. 2/6 and 2/-.
A Sister's Sin. 2/6 and 2/-.
Weak Woman. 2/6 and 2/-.
A Daughter's Heart. 2/6 and 2/-.
A Lost Wife. 2/6 and 2/-.
Jack's Secret. 2/6 and 2/-.
In a Grass Country. 1/- and 3/6.
The Man Who Didn't. 1/- and 1/6.

14 BEDFORD STREET, STRAND, W.C.

CROKER (B. M.)
A Third Person. 2/6 and 2/-. | Interference. 2/6 and 2/-.

CROMMELIN (MAY)
The Freaks of Lady Fortune. 2/6 and 2/-.

CROMMELIN (MAY) & BROWN (J. MORAY)
Violet Vyvian, M.F.H. 2/6 and 2/-.

CALMOUR (ALFRED)
The Confessions of a Door Mat. 1/- and 1/6.

DAY (WILLIAM)
Turf Celebrities I Have Known. 16/-.

FENN (GEORGE MANVILLE)
Cursed by a Fortune. 6/-. | The Case of Ailsa Gray. 6/-.

FARJEON (B. L.)
The March of Fate. 2/6 and 2/-. | A Young Girl's Life. 2/6 and 2/-.
Basil and Annette. 2/6 and 2/-. | Toilers of Babylon. 2/6 and 2/-.

FRASER (Mrs ALEXANDER)
A Modern Bridegroom. 2/-.

FETHERSTONHAUGH (The Honourable Mrs)
Dream Faces. 2/6.

GRIFFITH (GEORGE)
Briton or Boer ? (Illustrated.) 3/6.

GROSSMITH (WEEDON)
A Woman with a History. 1/- and 1/6.

GRIMWOOD (Mrs FRANK ST CLAIR)
The Power of an Eye. 1/- and 1/6.

GOWING (Mrs AYLMER)

Gods of Gold. 6/-.

GARLE (HUBERT)

Hunting in the Golden Days. (Illustrated.) 3/6.

HENTY (G. A.)

A Woman of the Commune. A Tale of Two Sieges of Paris. (Illustrated.) 6/-.

HUNGERFORD (Mrs)

A Tug of War. 2/6.
Peter's Wife. 2/6 and 2/-.
The Hon. Mrs Vereker. 2/6 and 2/-.

HUMBERT (MABEL)

Continental Chit Chat. 1/-.

HUME (FERGUS)

The Man with a Secret. 2/6 and 2/-.
The Gentleman Who Vanished. 1/- and 1/6.
The Piccadilly Puzzle. 1/- and 1/6.
Miss Mephistopheles. 1/-.

HUMPHRY (Mrs) ("MADGE," of *Truth*)

Housekeeping. 3/6.

JOCELYN (Mrs ROBERT)

For One Season Only. A Sporting Novel. 2/6 and 2/-.

A Regular Fraud. 2/6 and 2/-.	Drawn Blank. 2/6 and 2/-.
Only a Horse Dealer. 2/6 and 2/-.	The Criton Hunt Mystery. 2/6 and 2/-.
A Big Stake. 2/6 and 2/-.	The M.F.H.'s Daughter. 2/6 and 2/-.

KENNARD (Mrs EDWARD)

A Riverside Romance. 6/- & 2/6.
Fooled by a Woman. 2/6.
The Plaything of an Hour, and other Stories. 2/6 and 2/-.
The Catch of the County. 2/6 and 2/-.
Wedded to Sport. 3/6 and 2/-.
The Hunting Girl. 2/6 and 2/-.
Just Like a Woman. 2/6 and 2/-.
Sporting Tales. 2/6 and 2/-.
Twilight Tales. (Illustrated.) 2/6.
That Pretty Little Horsebreaker. 2/6 and 2/-.
Straight as a Die. 2/6 and 2/-.

Matron or Maid? 2/6 and 2/-.
A Crack County. 2/6 and 2/-.
Landing a Prize. 2/6 and 2/-.
A Homburg Beauty. 2/6 and 2/-.
Our Friends in the Hunting Field. 2/6 and 2/-.
The Mystery of a Woman's Heart. 1/- and 1/6.
The Sorrows of a Golfer's Wife. 2/6.
A Guide Book for Lady Cyclists. 1/- and 1/6.
The Girl in the Brown Habit. 3/6. (Illustrated.)

LE QUEUX (WILLIAM)

Devil's Dice. 6/-.

LITTLE (Mrs ARCHIBALD)

A Marriage in China. 6/-.

MEADE (Mrs L. T.)

A Son of Ishmael. 6/-.

McMILLAN (Mrs ALEC)

The Evolution of Daphne. 6/-.

MATHERS (HELEN)

A Man of To-day. 2/6 and 2/-.

MARRYAT (FLORENCE)

The Spirit World. 2/6 and 2/-.

MACGREGOR (Surgeon-Major)

Through the Buffer State: a Record of Recent Travels through Borneo, Siam and Cambodia. With Ten whole-page Illustrations and a Map. 6/-.

MURRAY (DAVID CHRISTIE)

The Investigations of John Pym. 1/- and 1/6.

NISBET (HUME)

The Swampers. (Illustrated.) 3/6.
The Rebel Chief. 3/6.
A Desert Bride. 3/6 and 2/-.
A Bushgirl's Romance. 3/6 & 2/-.

The Queen's Desire. 3/6 and 2/-.
The Great Secret. 2/6 and 2/-.
The Haunted Station. 2/6.
My Love Noel. 2/6 and 2/-.

PRAED (Mrs CAMPBELL)

The Romance of a Chalet. 2/6 and 2/-.

PHILIPS (F. C.)

The Luckiest of Three. 1/- and 1/6. | A Devil in Nun's Veiling. 1/- and 1/6.

PHILIPS (F. C.), and PERCY FENDALL

My Face is My Fortune. 2/6 and 2/-. | A Daughter's Sacrifice. 2/6 and 2/-.
Margaret Byng. 2/6.

PHILIPS (F. C.), and C. J. WILLS

Sybil Ross's Marriage. 2/6 and 2/-.

"RITA."

Vignettes. 6/-.
Joan & Mrs Carr. 6/-. and 2/6.
The Man in Possession. 2/6 & 2/-.
The Laird of Cockpen. 2/6 & 2/-.

The Countess Pharamond. 2/6.
Miss Kate. 2/6 and 2/-.
Naughty Mrs Gordon. 1/- and 1/6.
The Seventh Dream. 1/- and 1/6.

Sheba. 2/6.

ROBERTS (MORLEY)

The Courage of Pauline. 1/- and 1/6.

RIDDELL (Mrs J. H.)

A Silent Tragedy. 1/- and 1/6.

ROBERTS (Sir RANDAL, Bart.)

Not in the Betting. 2/6. | Handicapped. 2/6 and 2/-.
Curb and Snaffle. 2/6.

SIMS (G. R.)

As it Was in the Beginning. 2/6. | The Coachman's Club. 2/6.

ST AUBYN (ALAN)

A Proctor's Wooing. 6/-.
To Step Aside is Human. 2/6.

A Tragic Honeymoon. 2/.
In the Sweet West Country. 2/6 and 2/.

STUART (ESMÈ)

Arrested. 6/-.

SMART (HAWLEY)

A Racing Rubber. 2/6 and 2/-.

SERGEANT (ADELINE)

Told in the Twilight. 6/- and 2/6.

THOMAS (ANNIE)

Four Women in the Case. 6/-.

Essentially Human. 6/-.

WARDEN (FLORENCE)

Our Widow. 6/-.
A Lady in Black. 6/- and 2/6.
Dr Darch's Wife. 2/6.
A Spoilt Girl. 2/6.
A Perfect Fool. 2/6 and 2/-.
Strictly Incog. 2/6 and 2/-.
My Child and I. 2/6 and 2/-.
A Wild Wooing. 2/6 and 2/-.
A Witch of the Hills. 2/6 and 2/-.

The Mystery of Dudley Horne. 6/-.
A Young Wife's Trial. 2/6 and 2/-.
Kitty's Engagement. 2/6 and 2/-.
A Woman's Face. 2/-.
The Woman with the Diamonds. 1/- and 1/6.
A Scarborough Romance. 1/- and 1/6.
Two Lads and a Lass. 1/- and 1/6.

WINTER (JOHN STRANGE)

Into an Unknown World. 6/-.
The Strange Story of my Life. 6/-.
The Truth Tellers. 6/-.
A Magnificent Young Man. 2/6.
A Blameless Woman. 2/6.
A Born Soldier. 2/6 and 2/-.
A Seventh Child. 2/6 and 2/-.
The Soul of the Bishop. 2/6 and 2/-.
Aunt Johnnie. 2/6 and 2/-.
My Geoff. 2/6 and 2/-.

Only Human. 2/6 and 2/-.
The Other Man's Wife. 2/6 and 2/-.
Army Society. 2/-.
A Siege Baby. 2/6 and 2/-.
Beautiful Jim. 2/6 and 2/-.
Garrison Gossip. 2/6 and 2/-.
Mrs Bob. 2/6 and 2/-.
The Troubles of an Unlucky Boy. 1/- and 1/6.
Grip. 1/- and 1/6.

WINTER (JOHN STRANGE)—*continued*

I Loved Her Once. 1/- and 1/6.

The Same Thing with a Difference. 1/- and 1/6-.

I Married a Wife. (Profusely Illustrated.) 1/- and 1/6.

Private Tinker; and other Stories. (Profusely Illustrated.) 1/- and 1/6.

The Major's Favourite. 1/- and 1/6.

The Stranger Woman. 1/- and 1/6.

Red Coate. (Profusely Illustrated.) 1/- and 1/6.

A Man's Man. 1/- and 1/6.

That Mrs Smith. 1/- and 1/6.

Three Girls. 1/- and 1/6.

Mere Luck. 1/- and 1/6.

Lumley the Painter. 1/- and 1/6.

Good-Bye. 1/- and 1/6.

He Went for a Soldier. 1/- and 1/6.

Ferrers Court. 1/- and 1/6.

A Little Fool. 1/- and 1/6.

Buttons. 1/- and 1/6.

Bootles' Children. (Illustrated.) 1/- and 1/6.

The Confessions of a Publisher. 1/- and 1/6.

My Poor Dick. (Illustrated.) 1/- and 1/6.

That Imp. 1/- and 1/6.

Mignon's Secret. 1/- and 1/6.

Mignon's Husband. 1/- and 1/6.

On March. 1/- and 1/6.

In Quarters. 1/- and 1/6.

YOLLAND (E.)

In Days of Strife. 6/-.

SIX SHILLING NOVELS

In One Vol., Cloth Gilt, Price 6s. each

INTO AN UNKNOWN WORLD. By JOHN STRANGE WINTER.

THE MYSTERY OF DUDLEY HORNE. By FLORENCE WARDEN.

THE EVOLUTION OF DAPHNE. By Mrs ALEC McMILLAN.

ESSENTIALLY HUMAN. By ANNIE THOMAS.

THE STRANGE STORY OF MY LIFE. By JOHN STRANGE WINTER.

A SPLENDID SIN. By GRANT ALLEN.

DEVIL'S DICE. By WILLIAM LE QUEUX.

CURSED BY A FORTUNE. By G. MANVILLE FENN.

A GOLDEN AUTUMN. By Mrs ALEXANDER.

A PROCTOR'S WOOING. By ALAN ST AUBYN.

GODS OF GOLD. By Mrs AYLMER-GOWING.

A MARRIAGE IN CHINA. By Mrs ARCHIBALD LITTLE.

ARRESTED. By ESMÈ STUART.

A SON OF ISHMAEL. By Mrs L. T. MEADE.

VIGNETTES. By "RITA."

FOUR WOMEN IN THE CASE. By ANNIE THOMAS.

TRUTH TELLERS. By JOHN STRANGE WINTER.

A WOMAN OF THE COMMUNE. By G. A. HENTY. (Illustrated.)

MARLBOROUGH HOUSE AND ITS OCCUPANTS, PRESENT
I AND PAST. By ARTHUR H. BEAVAN. With 16 full-page Illustrations.

IN DAYS OF STRIFE. By E. YOLLAND.

OUR WIDOW. By FLORENCE WARDEN.

THE CASE OF AILSA GRAY. By GEORGE MANVILLE FENN.

JOAN & MRS CARR. By "RITA."

TOLD IN THE TWILIGHT. By ADELINE SERGEANT.

A RIVERSIDE ROMANCE. By Mrs EDWARD KENNARD.

A LADY IN BLACK. By FLORENCE WARDEN.

THROUGH THE BUFFER STATE: A Record of Recent Travels
    through Borneo, Siam and Cambodia. By Surgeon-Major MACGREGOR,
    M.D. Ten whole-page Illustrations and a Map.

Novels at Three Shillings and Sixpence

In One Vol., Cloth Gilt, Price 3s. 6d. each

The Swampers. By HUME NISBET. (Illustrated.)

In a Grass Country. By Mrs LOVETT CAMERON. (With Frontispiece.)

Briton or Boer? By GEORGE GRIFFITH. (Illustrated.)

The Girl in the Brown Habit. By Mrs EDWARD KENNARD. (With Frontispiece.)

Two Cousins and a Castle. By Mrs LOVETT CAMERON.

The Rebel Chief. By HUME NISBET. (Illustrated by the Author.)

A Desert Bride: a Story of Adventure in India and Persia. By HUME NISBET. (With Illustrations by the Author.)

A Bush Girl's Romance. By HUME NISBET. (With Illustrations by the Author.)

Wedded to Sport. By Mrs EDWARD KENNARD.

Housekeeping; a Guide to Domestic Management. By Mrs HUMPHRY ("Madge," of *Truth*.)

The Queen's Desire: a Romance of the Indian Mutiny. By HUME NISBET. (With Illustrations by the Author.)

Hunting in the Golden Days. By HUBERT GARLE. (Illustrated by FINCH MASON.)

Novels at Two Shillings and Sixpence

In One Vol., Cloth, Price 2s. 6s. each

A Magnificent Young Man. By JOHN STRANGE WINTER.

A Blameless Woman. By the same Author.

A Born Soldier. By the same Author.

The Soul of the Bishop. By the same Author.

A Seventh Child. By the same Author.

Aunt Johnnie. By the same Author.

The Other Man's Wife. By the same Author.

Beautiful Jim. By the same Author.

Garrison Gossip. By the same Author.

My Geoff. By the same Author.

Only Human. By the same Author.

Mrs Bob. By the same Author.

A Siege Baby. By JOHN STRANGE WINTER.
As it Was in the Beginning. By GEO. R. SIMS.
The Coachman's Club. By the same Author.
Dr Darch's Wife. By FLORENCE WARDEN.
A Spoilt Girl. By the same Author.
The Sorrows of a Golfer's Wife. By Mrs EDWARD KENNARD.
A Man of To-Day. By HELEN MATHERS.
A Racing Rubber. By HAWLEY SMART.
A Third Person. By B. M. CROKER.
Interference. By the same Author.
The Man With a Secret. By FERGUS HUME.
Basil and Annette. By B. L. FARJEON.
The March of Fate. By the same Author.
A Young Girl's Life. By the same Author.
Toilers of Babylon. By the same Author.
The Catch of the County. By Mrs EDWARD KENNARD.
Fooled by a Woman. By the same Author.
The Plaything of an Hour, and Other Stories. By the same Author.
That Pretty Little Horsebreaker. By the same Author.
The Hunting Girl. By the same Author.
Just Like a Woman. By the same Author.
Sporting Tales. By the same Author.
Twilight Tales. By the same Author. (Illustrated.)
A Homburg Beauty. By the same Author.
Landing a Prize. By the same Author.
A Crack County. By the same Author.
Our Friends in the Hunting Field. By the same Author.
Straight as a Die. By the same Author.
A Riverside Romance. By the same Author.
Matron or Maid? By the same Author.
Little Lady Lee. By Mrs LOVETT CAMERON.
A Soul Astray. By the same Author.
A Bad Lot. By the same Author.
A Daughter's Heart. By the same Author.
A Tragic Blunder. By the same Author.
A Bachelor's Bridal. By the same Author.
A Sister's Sin. By the same Author.
Jack's Secret. By the same Author.
Weak Woman. By the same Author.
A Lost Wife. By the same Author.
A Choice of Evils. By Mrs ALEXANDER.
What Gold Cannot Buy. By the same Author.
Found Wanting. By the same Author.
For His Sake. By the same Author.
A Woman's Heart. By the same Author.
The Laird o' Cockpen. By "RITA."
Joan & Mrs Carr. By the same Author.
Sheba; a Study of Girlhood. By the same Author.
The Countess Pharamond; A Sequel to "Sheba." By the same Author.
The Man in Possession. By the same Author.

Miss Kate.   By "RITA."
The Romance of a Chalet.   By Mrs CAMPBELL-PRAED.
The Freaks of Lady Fortune.   By MAY CROMMELIN.
Violet Vyvian, M.F.H.   By MAY CROMMELIN and J. MORAY BROWN.
Peter's Wife.   By Mrs HUNGERFORD.
A Tug of War.   By the same Author.
The Hon. Mrs Vereker.   By the same Author.
Dream Faces.   By THE Hon. Mrs FETHERSTONHAUGH.
Handicapped.   By Sir RANDAL H. ROBERTS, Bart.
Curb and Snaffle.   By the same Author.
Not in the Betting.   By the same Author.
Sybil Ross's Marriage.   By F. C. PHILIPS and C. J. WILLS.
My Face is my Fortune.   By F. C. PHILIPS and PERCY FENDALL.
Margaret Byng.   By the same Authors.
A Daughter's Sacrifice.   By the same Authors.
A Regular Fraud.   By Mrs ROBERT JOCELYN.
The Criton Hunt Mystery.   By the same Author.
For one Season Only.   (A Sporting Novel.)   By the same Author.
Only a Horse Dealer.   By the same Author.
A Big Stake.   By the same Author.
Drawn Blank.   By the same Author.
The M.F.H.'s Daughter.   By the same Author.
Kitty's Engagement.   By FLORENCE WARDEN.
A Perfect Fool.   By the same Author.
Strictly Incog; being the Record of a Passage through Bohemia.   By the
      same Author.
A Lady in Black.   By the same Author.
A Wild Wooing.   By the same Author.
My Child and I.   A Woman's Story.   By the same Author.
A Young Wife's Trial; or Ralph Ryder of Brent.   By the same Author.
A Witch of the Hills.   By the same Author.
My Love Noel.   By HUME NISBET.
The Great Secret; A Tale of To-morrow.   By the same Author.
The Haunted Station; and other Stories.   By the same Author.
The Spirit World.   By FLORENCE MARRYAT.
To Step Aside is Human.   By ALAN ST AUBYN.
In the Sweet West Country.   By the same Author.
Told in the Twilight.   By ADELINE SERGEANT.

NOVELS AT TWO SHILLINGS.

In Picture Boards, Price 2s. each.

A Born Soldier. By JOHN STRANGE WINTER.
A Bad Lot. By Mrs LOVETT CAMERON.
Handicapped. By Sir RANDAL ROBERTS, Bart.
The Spirit World. By FLORENCE MARRYAT.
In the Sweet West Country. By ALAN ST AUBYN.
The Great Secret. By HUME NISBET. | My Love Noel. By the same Author.
A Seventh Child. By JOHN STRANGE WINTER.
The Soul of the Bishop. By the same Author.
Aunt Johnnie. By the same Author. | My Geoff. By the same Author.
Only Human. By the same Author. | Mrs Bob. By the same Author.
The Other Man's Wife. By the same Author.
Beautiful Jim. By the same Author.
A Siege Baby. By the same Author.
Garrison Gossip. By the same Author.
Army Society; Life in a Garrison Town. By the same Author.
A Man of To-day. By HELEN MATHERS.
A Man with a Secret. By FERGUS HUME.
A Racing Rubber. By HAWLEY SMART.
What Gold Cannot Buy. By Mrs ALEXANDER.
Found Wanting. By the same Author.
A Woman's Heart. By the same Author.
For His Sake. By the same Author. | A Third Person. By B. M. CROKER.
A Choice of Evils. By the same Author. | Interference. By the same Author.
Peter's Wife. By Mrs HUNGERFORD.
The Hon. Mrs Vereker. By the same Author.
Sporting Tales. By Mrs EDWARD KENNARD.
The Catch of the County. By the same Author.
The Hunting Girl. By the same Author.
Just Like a Woman. By the same Author.
Matron or Maid? By the same Author.
Wedded to Sport. By the same Author.
That Pretty Little Horsebreaker. By the same Author.
A Homburg Beauty. By the same Author.
Our Friends in the Hunting-Field. By the same Author.
Landing a Prize. By the same Author.
A Crack County. By the same Author.
Straight as a Die. By the same Author.

The Plaything of an Hour. By Mrs EDWARD KENNARD.
A Tragic Blunder. By Mrs LOVETT CAMERON.
Little Lady Lee. By the same Author.
A Bachelor's Bridal. By the same Author.
A Daughter's Heart. By the same Author.
A Lost Wife. By the same Author.
Weak Woman. By the same Author.
A Sister's Sin. By the same Author.
Jack's Secret. By the same Author.
The March of Fate. By B. L. FARJEON.
Toilers of Babylon. By the same Author.
Basil and Annette. By the same Author.
A Young Girl's Life. By the same Author.
Strictly Incog. By FLORENCE WARDEN.
A Perfect Fool. By the same Author.
My Child and I: A Woman's Story. By the same Author.
A Woman's Face. By the same Author.
A Young Wife's Trial; or, Ralph Ryder of Brent. By the same Author.
A Wild Wooing. By the same Author.
A Witch of the Hills. By the same Author.
Kitty's Engagement. By the same Author.
The Man in Possession. By "Rita."
Miss Kate. By the same Author.
The Laird o' Cockpen. By the same Author.
A Modern Bridegroom. By Mrs ALEXANDER FRASER.
The Romance of a Chalet. By Mrs CAMPBELL-PRAED.
Violet Vyvian, M.F.H. By MAY CROMMELIN and J. MORAY BROWN.
The Freaks of Lady Fortune. By MAY CROMMELIN.
Sybil Ross's Marriage. By F. C. PHILIPS and C. J. WILLS.
My Face is My Fortune. By F. C. PHILIPS and PERCY FENDALL.
A Daughter's Sacrifice. By the same Authors.
A Desert Bride. By HUME NISBET.
A Bush Girl's Romance. By the same Author.
The Queen's Desire. By the same Author.
Drawn Blank. By Mrs ROBERT JOCELYN.
For One Season Only: a Sporting Novel. By the same Author.
The M.F.H.'s Daughter. By the same Author.
Only a Horse Dealer. By the same Author.
A Big Stake. By the same Author.
The Criton Hunt Mystery. By the same Author.
A Regular Fraud. By the same Author.
A Tragic Honeymoon. By ALAN ST AUBYN.

ONE SHILLING NOVELS

In Paper Covers.   Also in Cloth, 1s. 6d.

The Troubles of an Unlucky Boy. By JOHN STRANGE WINTER.
Grip. By the same Author.
The Same Thing with a Difference. By the same Author.
I Loved Her Once. By the same Author.
I Married a Wife. By the same Author.
Private Tinker, and Other Stories. By the same Author. (Illustrated.)
The Major's Favourite. By the same Author.
The Stranger Woman. By the same Author.
Red Coats. By the same Author. | A Man's Man. By the same Author.
That Mrs Smith. By the same Author.
Three Girl's. By the same Author. | Mere Luck. By the same Author.
Lumley the Painter. By the same Author.
Good-bye. By the same Author.
He Went for a Soldier. By the same Author.
Ferrers Court. By the same Author. | Buttons. By the same Author.
A Little Fool. By the same Author.
My Poor Dick. By the same Author. (Illustrated by MAURICE GREIFFEN-
    HAGEN.)
Bootles' Children. By the same Author. (Illustrated by J. BERNARD
    PARTRIDGE.)
The Confessions of a Publisher. By the same Author.
Mignon's Husband. By the same Author.
That Imp. By the same Author. | Mignon's Secret. By the same Author.
On March. By the same Author. | In Quarters. By the same Author.
The Courage of Pauline. By MORLEY ROBERTS.
A Woman with a History. By WEEDON GROSSMITH.
A Devil in Nun's Veiling. By F. C. PHILIPS.
The Luckiest of Three. By the same Author.
The Investigations of John Pym. By DAVID CHRISTIE MURRAY.
A Silent Tragedy. By Mrs J. H. RIDDELL.
The Power of an Eye. By Mrs FRANK ST CLAIR GRIMWOOD.
The Gentleman Who Vanished. By FERGUS HUME.
Miss Mephistopheles. By the same Author.
The Piccadilly Puzzle. By the same Author.
The Man Who Didn't. By Mrs LOVETT CAMERON.
In a Grass Country; a Story of Love and Sport. By the same Author.
The Confessions of a Door Mat. By ALFRED C. CALMOUR.
The Mystery of a Woman's Heart. By Mrs EDWARD KENNARD.
A Guide Book for Lady Cyclists. By the same Author.
The Woman with the Diamonds. By FLORENCE WARDEN.
Two Lads and a Lass. By the same Author.
City and Suburban. By the same Author.
A Scarborough Romance. By the same Author.
Naughty Mrs Gordon; a Romance of Society. By "RITA."
The Seventh Dream. By the same Author.
A Mad Prank. By Mrs HUNGERFORD.
Continental Chit Chat. By MABEL HUMBERT.

The Welcome Library

(With which is incorporated "THE MODERN NOVELIST")

A NEW MONTHLY SERIES OF FICTION...
...BY POPULAR AUTHORS

IN PAPER COVERS, 3d. each

By DORA RUSSELL, Author of "Footprints in the Snow"

1. **FOR THE CHILD'S SAKE**

By MRS HUNGERFORD, Author of "Molly Bawn"

2. **A CONQUERING HEROINE**

By MRS ALEXANDER FRASER

3. **SHE CAME BETWEEN**

By LADY CONSTANCE HOWARD

4. **SWEETHEART AND WIFE**

By FLORENCE MARRYAT

5. **FOR A WOMAN'S PLEASURE**

By ANNIE THOMAS

6. **BLUE EYES AND GOLDEN HAIR**

By JEAN MIDDLEMASS

7. **ALL FOR LOVE**

By ANNIE THOMAS

8. **THE OLD LOVE AGAIN**

By MRS HUNGERFORD

9. **HER LAST THROW**

⇥ OTHERS TO FOLLOW ⇤

14 BEDFORD STREET, STRAND, W.C.

9 783337 049041